Cop

CW01475807

Th.

The characters and events portrayed in this book are fictitious. Any similarity to real persons, living or dead, is coincidental and not intended by the author.

No part of this book may be reproduced, or stored in a retrieval system, or transmitted in any form or by any means, electronic, mechanical, photocopying, recording, or otherwise, without express written permission of the publisher.

ISBN: 978-1-0684483-3-1

Published by Simon A Ford - simonafordpublish@gmail.com

# The Woodland Path Murders

## Author's Forward

I have used a little literary licence in the telling of the following story, both in terms of characters, and places where they play out the action. The settings are broadly based on fact but to fit the story I have embellished or altered them slightly. I ask for the forgiveness of any locals, purists or historians who may take offence at this.

## Introduction

For centuries there has been a huge amount of research and as a result, much written about, the human brain and the associated mind. The concept of a 'normal' mind or person is too simplistic. There are so many variations to character, both from cultural and societal influence and sometimes just organic, that it is virtually impossible to standardise the definition. The nature versus nurture argument is still raging among some experts.

The human brain has been studied physiologically and psychologically for millennia. We still can't truly say that we understand it fully, by any measure. It used to be thought that humans only utilise about 10% of the potential capacity of the brain. This is now thought to be a myth and we actually use all of it, even during sleep. It is a complex organ, made up of 60% fat, weighs about 3lbs and has billions of neutrons that store information (capacity thought to be almost limitless) and trillions of synapses that communicate between them, at speeds of up to 350 miles per hour.

Think of the amazing things that the human race has achieved over thousands of years. The engineering, the art, the music, the medicine and science in general. Our understanding of the world we live in has progressed massively due to the collective cooperation of people whose brains have mastered learning and understanding.

It's no wonder that sometimes things go wrong, bits might not develop properly or may get damaged due to trauma, both physical and emotional.

Illnesses of the brain are also more understood nowadays. We have moved on, in the main, from the fear of people who are different, whether that be on a physical or mental basis. No longer are they cast aside or locked up away from society. We try to treat them and help them to fit in and lead a better life.

This isn't always possible, of course. There are still people who we might label as evil. Sociopaths and Psychopaths can fall into that category. They are now referred to as having Antisocial Personality Disorder or APD. One of the major things that people like this lack is empathy, which is such an important trait of someone we might call 'normal'.

Treatment of people who suffer from APD has gone through many guises from solitary confinement, physical abuse, crude surgical interventions and electric shock therapy. Drugs are now more commonly used to control patients but there is no cure for APD. In extreme circumstance, of course, society will still lock up people who are dangerous or who have committed an atrocity. In some parts of the world the Death Penalty is still used.

Of course, not all people with APD become killers. Some are considered to be successful people, perhaps in business or politics.

The above paragraphs in themselves are a very simplified version of current understandings but are meant as an introduction to how and why people do the some of the things they do, as background for this book. For those of us who consider ourselves to be 'normal' we should just reflect on history and see the contrasts between the good and bad that the human race has done. And this has not just been individuals but includes things done in the name of Countries, States and some Religions. Should we study closer the people we allow to run our lives? If we look at the actions of some world leaders even today, let alone throughout history, we have to wonder about the state of their minds, surely.

**Extract from Warwick Town Council web page**

There is evidence of human activity at Warwick as early as the Neolithic age, and of constant habitation since the 6th century. A Saxon fort was created in Warwick in 914 AD as a defence against the Danes, and **Warwick Castle** was established in 1068 AD as part of the Norman conquest of England.

The earldom of Warwick was created in 1088

and the earls controlled the town in the medieval period. During this time Warwick was given town walls of which only Eastgate and Westgate survive. The castle developed into a stone fortress and then a country house and is today a popular tourist attraction.

The Great Fire of Warwick in 1694 destroyed much of the medieval town and as a result most of the buildings post-date this period. Also as a consequence of the fire, thatched roofing was banned from the town.

Warwick continues to be the heart of Warwickshire, its County town and the base for the County Council.

## Prologue

*Ten Years ago*

This would be his first….his first human at any rate. He had plenty of practice on small furry animals, rabbits, cats, small birds. Now it was time to graduate. To move up the scale to his fellow human beings. He tingled with anticipation.

The designated victim was unknown to him, though he had spent a little time watching and following the man. One had to gauge the physical attributes of the prey and make sure they were likely to be weaker than oneself. It made sense.

The man in his sights was slight of build, average height and seemed hesitant around other people. Weak, he surmised, both in stature and in character. Shouldn't be difficult to overpower. Not having done this before, the hunter was slightly nervous. Had he got it right about the man? No point in wasting more time. It was dark, nobody else around, back street, dimly lit. Ideal.

He had been following in the shadows for a little while, down the back streets of Warwick. It was an area of terraced Victorian properties, all in a straight line. Probably built as workers houses originally. Several roads with interconnecting pathways. What street lighting there was didn't do a great job, part of the reason he chose the scene. He looked around one last time to make sure no one else was likely to disturb him. All clear. Time to pounce.

He quickened his pace and caught up with the man.

"Excuse me mate, have you got a light by any chance?" he enquired, in as friendly a manner as he could manage.

"Err, yeah....sure" said the man, hesitantly. As he reached into his pocket, the hunter leaped at him, taking him off guard. Hands around the throat, stifling the alarmed scream. Fear and disbelief in the man's eyes as the hunter tightened his grip around the man's windpipe.

The struggling was getting weaker, not that it

had been strong in the first place. This was going to be easy. And delicious.

"Oi" came a loud shout from some way down the street. "What's going on?"

The hunter swivelled and saw the obvious outline of a copper in the distance. Said copper began to run towards them.

"Shit" said the hunter. He loosened his grip and the man crumpled to the ground. The hunter then legged it as fast as he could and shot off up a footpath that led to a large park surrounded by woods. His adrenalin was already flowing and now his flight instinct also kicked in. He quickly disappeared into the darkness.

The policeman got to the crumpled man and established that he was incapacitated but still alive. He had seen that the other man had been trying to strangle him.

He called in for back up and an ambulance, both of which took some 15 minutes to arrive. There was no way he could give chase and leave this man in a heap on the ground. He was still alive but unable to speak. His windpipe was all but crushed and in the lamplight, his face was a strange colour. All the policeman could do was to cradle the man in his arms, crouched on the ground, and wait for help to arrive.

The man was taken to hospital and the policeman and a couple of colleagues did a search of the area but found nothing. The attacker was long gone.

Two days later the man was deemed fit by the hospital to be able to answer some questions. The PC visited him in the hospital and asked a few questions but the man was unable to help, other than a vague description of his attacker. He didn't know him and had no idea why he had been attacked.

He had been amazingly lucky that the policeman had come along when he did. The local newspaper picked up the story and the following appeared:

*Mystery attacker thwarted by local hero bobby.*

*Police Constable Chamberlain was on routine patrol when he saw a man being attacked. Without hesitation, he ran to the man's assistance, scaring off the attacker and saving the man's life. If anyone saw anything or knows any more information, please get in touch with the local police or contact the National Crime Line.*

The hunter, now safely out of the area, was furious. Seeing the newspaper made it even worse. That name, Chamberlain, would be remembered. He would get his revenge one day. He was not a forgiving person and had a long memory. It had been going so well, only a few moments and the man would have been dead.

He could already see the flaws in his plan.

He had thought they wouldn't be disturbed but he was clearly wrong. Next time he would choose the location more wisely. Somewhere no one would be when he was executing his project. Somewhere rural maybe. Woods. Yes, under the cover of darkness. The complication would be getting his prey to the location. He would work it out. He was methodical. And eventually he would get that bastard copper. Said copper was basking in the glory of his heroic feat.

Actually the policeman didn't really think of himself as a hero. He was doing his job. However, the attention would do his professional record no harm. He had ambitions and positive things that got him noticed by the hierarchy were no bad thing. He had his sights set on CID. He knew he would have to work hard for it and it may take a few years to get there but he could definitely see himself as a Detective Inspector.

He was right and the attention did him no harm at all. Within a year he transferred out of the area to Bristol CID as a Detective Constable. He was involved in all sorts of investigations, drug gangs, domestic violence and murder. He did his sergeants exams and became a detective Sergeant

He was known, within the range of close colleagues, as the quirky detective, due to the pipe he was always puffing on, outside the office at any rate.

It wasn't long before the top brass noticed him and wanted to put him somewhere as a DI. Nothing came up for a couple of years until there was a retirement and a promotion which meant there was a position available at Warwick CID. Back on home ground. Chamberlain took the position without hesitation.

# CHAPTER 1

*Present Day*

The way an owl hunts at night relies very much on their enhanced senses. By which is meant eyesight and hearing, in the main. Woodland owls often perch-hunt (looking and listening for prey) and follow regular routes through the trees, effectively flying blind, guided towards noisy quarry by acoustic cues. Owls are silent fliers thanks to their specially designed wing feathers that muffle the air, allowing them to swoop down unheard.

They do much of their hunting with the aid of their incredible hearing. Owl hearing has been most extensively studied in Barn Owls. These pale predators can see very well in low light, but their ears are better. Their hearing is the best of any animal that has ever been tested.

When a fox hunts at night they also rely on these same senses but also a large amount of stealth. They hunt by stalking their live prey. They have excellent hearing and use a pouncing technique that allows them to kill the prey quickly. They listen for animals moving underground or under the snow in winter and use a combination of pouncing and digging to get to it.

When a psychopathic killer hunts, day or night, they usually rely on very good planning or an MO (Modus Operandi) as it is referred to by psychologists, criminologists and the police.

They talk about apex killers/hunters in the animal kingdom but really the top of the pile is the human and in particular, the psychopath. If you saw one in the street you wouldn't necessarily know what they were. However, more than cursory contact and you would start to see the signs. These could be some or all of a damning list - behaviour that conflicts with social norms, disregarding or violating the rights of others, inability to distinguish between right and wrong, difficulty with showing remorse or empathy, manipulating and hurting others.

Sociopath is an outdated, informal term for someone who has antisocial personality disorder (APD). This disorder can cause you to lack empathy, which means you don't care about or understand other peoples' feelings and have a tendency to act on the spur of the moment whereas a psychopath is good at planning and the long game.

If you learn more about them you may find they have had recurring problems with the law, though they may be good at hiding this. Sometimes these traits are hidden well but it is just good acting. The Psychopath is a good actor and is very good at hiding many of his characteristics, which is why he has been so successful....at least in his eyes. One might call it purely evil.

Yes, no doubt it started when he was young... nature or nurture? A bit of both one could surmise. There must have been an organic seed to his journey. But then he was brought up in a very dysfunctional family where his mother was the controlling power over them all, including his weak father, as he saw him.

He couldn't remember either of them showing him any affection, either physical or emotional. Quite the opposite. They didn't seem to like him at all. His mother had never hit him but neither had she ever comforted him after a fall or other accident. His father was too weak to be anything other than the shadowy figure sitting in the corner in his armchair, agreeing to everything his wife said or did.

He had been bullied and hit at school...a lot. Physical bruises faded in time but the mental scars he picked up were with him still. The reasons for being bullied cited most often by children are physical appearance, race/ethnicity, gender, disability, religion, and sexual orientation. Some youth s engage in bullying behaviour due to a lack of understanding differences in backgrounds, cultures and other identity markers.

He was teased for his appearance. Uncut greasy hair and second hand school uniform made him an easy target for the other kids. He was also taller than most of his peers which literally made him stand out in a crowd. He also had bad personal hygiene, simply because he wasn't provided with the means to change this.

Eventually he was taken away from his biological family and went through a series of children's homes and then foster homes. He never really settled and in all cases the homes or families eventually found they could not cope with him. Then he ended up being taken on by a family who were experienced fosterers and who ended up adopting him.

They were functionally good parents but emotionally void, verging on inept. He was left to develop an already abnormal personality.

These are not excuses, maybe just some reasons for the way he is now. This night, he is hunting. He uses similar senses to the owl and fox and any deficiencies are boosted by technical means, like the powerful night vision binoculars he has hung by a strap around his neck.

He also has the advantage of having checked out his prey over an extended period of time, the last 6 weeks in fact. Yes, he had stalked him. He had pursued his prey with stealth, like the fox after his dinner, rather than the direct harassment and persecution that would have alerted his prey to what was developing.

So, the day, or rather the night, had arrived for the first part of the project. For he did view his 'adventures' as projects. To be researched diligently and then executed efficiently, and anonymously.

As he surveyed the landscape before him, a mixture of small patches of woodland interspersed with open fields, in front of a larger area of wood, easy to disappear into, he waited patiently in his foxhole. More of a shallow depression in the ground really but it was all that he needed to camouflage himself. He was dressed in dark clothing, not black, as he felt this could stand out more in semi dark conditions. Being in semi darkness had advantages and disadvantages but it was when he felt the most comfortable, not physically maybe but mentally. Being crouched in a damp piece of ground certainly became progressively less comfortable. He couldn't bring any kind of cushioning in case he had to move fast. It wouldn't do to leave anything behind in case it could be traced to him. They were so damn clever these days with their forensics.

He loved these patches of woodland and had played in them for hours as a youngster. Played in his definition, rather than most people. He would hunt anything that moved...and then kill it if he could catch it.

These woods were deciduous, mixed, mostly Beech, Oak and patches of Hazel. They used to be called Haseley, derived from the Saxon Haesel-leah meaning hazel wood, and the first record appears in 1086 in the Domesday Book. There was a Haseley Farm up the road but no one really called these woods anything anymore. No doubt they had been part of large forested areas hundreds, even thousands of years ago.

Where he lay, it smelled of rotting leaves and damp earth, mixed with the faint aroma of farm. Cow shit really. He was used to it, having spent a lot of his youth on a farm.

He spotted movement over to the left of his field of vision. Yes, there he was, the prey. It was ironic, he felt, that his prey was in fact hunting himself. Poaching to be more precise. Rabbits he would guess, maybe the odd fish out of the river that snaked across the landscape. He had no problem with people hurting or killing animals. He had done his fair share in the past. It had been his apprenticeship to what he was so good at now.

He would watch him for a while, delighting in the knowledge of what was to come. The deliciousness of knowing that his prey had no idea what was coming. It was worth hanging on to for a little longer.

Then...movement slightly away to the right of his prey. Was he poaching in company tonight? A slight, but not insurmountable addition to the nights' proceedings. He hadn't planned for this but he could adapt.

But wait, there was something strange about this seconded persons' movements. Could it be that he was following the prime prey covertly? The longer he watched the scene the clearer it became that this was indeed the case. The second figure would drop into cover if the first turned in their direction. This was interesting. Could it be that he had competition in his quest?

He supposed it was possible, though somewhat unlikely in his view. He would have to observe for a little longer. A strange kind of voyeurism. He became more and more fascinated with the scene unfolding before him. It felt weird but he found himself taking sides, with the original subject of his project. Who could this second hunter be?

The second hunter had no idea that his prey was also the prey of someone else. He wasn't a psychopath, more of a revengeful criminal.

If the prey had known he was the subject of interest to two hunters, he would have wished he had stayed in bed that day.

The prime hunter would have to think quickly. Yes, this would be an additional challenge, but if successful the result would be all the more delicious. It would also give his nemesis, Inspector Chamberlain of the Warwickshire Constabulary, something to think about.

His temporary refuge was just inside the tree line along the edge of what was about a ten acre field. It would soon be time to move. He was becoming more and more uncomfortable. He could taste the damp earth mixed with rotting leaves. He could, and probably should, have been angry at the interference with his meticulously planned project.

The ground on which he lay was becoming more uncomfortable with patches of damp starting to seep through his clothing. He had been lying here longer than planned now.

A new plan slowly began to emerge to the front of his mind and in the darkness he smiled. He didn't smile very often.

Prime    prey    supposedly    garrottes    second

hunter who stabs prime prey in the struggle....they both die. Both would have Means, Motive & Opportunity, even though it was engineered by an outside force. He would have to be careful to leave no trace of a third person's involvement. He saw a beauty in this scenario that appealed to his psychopathic mind.

# CHAPTER 2

Detective Inspector Ralph Chamberlain was sipping a cup of tea, sitting on a stool by the kitchen island, of which he was very proud. He was feeling fresh and full of vigour having just returned from some well earned annual leave. He wasn't a beach lounger. He travelled to places where he could investigate and enjoy different types of architecture and the history and culture behind it.

He had just got back from Barcelona in Northern Spain. He had learned about the early Roman town Barcino on which the current city was based. The Romans were great experts in civil architecture and engineering and provided roads, bridges, aqueducts and cities with a rational layout and basic services such as sewers.

But Barcelona's architectural gift to the world was Modernisme, a flamboyant Catalan creation that erupted in the late 19th century. Modernisme was personified by the visionary work of Antoni Gaudí, a giant in the world of architecture. Chamberlain had visited the Gaudi House Museum, located within the Park Güell in Barcelona. It is an historic home museum that houses a collection of furniture and objects designed by the Spanish architect. It was the residence of Antoni Gaudí for almost 20 years, from 1906 till the end of 1925.

He had been fascinated by the nature inspired design of the Casa Batlló and its facades that are shaped like natural corals, earning it the name 'House of Bones'. You can also see Gaud'ís use of colours and the chimney pots with the Trencadis artwork. This technique, pioneered by Gaudí, uses a mosaic of colourful ceramic tiles.

He had also visited the Gaudi Church or The Basílica i Temple Expiatori de Sagrada Família to give it it's full title, otherwise known as Sagrada Família, It is a church under construction in the Eixample district of Barcelona, Catalonia, Spain. It is the largest unfinished Catholic church in the world. Designed by Catalan architect Antoni Gaudí (1852–1926), in 2005 his work on Sagrada Família was added to an existing (1984) UNESCO World Heritage Site, "Works of Antoni Gaudí". On 7 November 2010, Pope Benedict XVI consecrated the church and proclaimed it a minor basilica.

On 19 March 1882, construction of Sagrada Família began under architect Francisco de Paula del Villar. In 1883, when Villar resigned, Gaudí took over as chief architect, transforming the project with his architectural and engineering style, combining Gothic and curvilinear Art Nouveau forms. Gaudí devoted the remainder of his life to the project, and he is buried in the church's crypt. At the time of his death in 1926, less than a quarter of the project was complete.

Relying solely on private donations, Sagrada Família's construction progressed slowly and was interrupted by the Spanish Civil War. In July 1936, anarchists from the FAI set fire to the crypt and broke their way into the workshop, partially destroying Gaudí's original plans. In 1939, Francesca de Paula Quintana took over site management, which was able to go on with the material that was saved from Gaudí's workshop and that was reconstructed from published plans and photographs. Construction resumed to intermittent progress in the 1950s. Advancements in technologies such as computer-aided design and computerised numerical control (CNC) have since enabled faster progress and construction passed the midpoint in 2010. In 2014, it was anticipated that the building would be completed by 2026, the centenary of Gaudí's death, but this schedule was threatened by work slowdowns caused by the 2020–2021 depths of the COVID-19 pandemic. In March 2024, an updated forecast reconfirmed a likely completion of the building in 2026, though the announcement stated that work on sculptures, decorative details and a controversial proposed stairway leading to what will eventually be the main entrance is expected to continue until 2034.

Describing Sagrada Família, art critic Rainer Zerbst said "it is probably impossible to find a church building anything like it in the entire history of art", and Paul Goldberger describes it as "the most extraordinary personal interpretation of Gothic architecture since the Middle Ages".

Though sometimes described as a cathedral, the basilica is not the cathedral church of the Archdiocese of Barcelona; that title belongs to the Cathedral of the Holy Cross and Saint Eulalia (Barcelona Cathedral).

Although not necessarily to his taste, Chamberlain could appreciate the pioneering designs that had made Gaudi such an influential and famous character.

He'd wanted to be a policeman from early on but if that hadn't worked out he would have studied to be an architect. How different his life would have been. He'd grown up in a reasonably happy family, not too much angst, not too much privilege. Luckier than some, not as well off as others. While he was growing up he hadn't really thought about it. It didn't occur to him that things were different for other people. His parents seemed happy and he assumed that was what happened when you grew up and got married.

Gradually he realised this wasn't always the case and there were levels to society, some much fairer than others. By the time he was a teenager he realised he had been viewing the world through rose tinted glasses. There were some bad things and bad people happening out there. *Not enough tolerance* he had always felt. Why couldn't people just like each other and get on?

As he learned more about how people were affected by their upbringing and surroundings be began to appreciate that it wasn't as simple as he first thought. Also, people were made differently, not always their own fault, sometimes organic, sometimes because of how they were brought up.

The human brain was so complicated. Underused, by all accounts. He started learning about people with damaged or differently made up brains. It didn't seem fair. He had veered away from any kind of religion or god as he felt it would be a pretty sick God who gave such pain to the human condition. Yeah, yeah, Pandora's Box and all that. Just stories to explain and to frighten, in his opinion. Control. People always wanted control of others.

So, one way he felt he could help society was to join the Police Force and help fight crime. There seemed to be enough of it about. Maybe he could balance the books to some degree.

Thoughts for another time, it was getting on and he had to get to the Supermarket for some supplies. It would be open late and he fancied something other than the basic supplies Mrs Frobisher, his housekeeper, had got in for him. It was a 20 minute drive under normal conditions but any kind of traffic issue and you could double that.

He checked that he had his pipe in his trouser pocket and his tin of Capstan Navy Cut pipe tobacco in his jacket pocket together with matches and keys. He preferred the use of matches as they tended not to taint the taste of the tobacco, unlike liquid or gas filled lighters.

He liked the mellow-bodied flake of the

Capstan tobacco. He had learned that he was in good company as J.R.R. Tolkien was also a fan of the brand.

He kept burning holes in his trouser pockets as he would put his pie in there without making sure it was out. It drove his housekeeper nuts as she kept having to patch the pockets. He had only two pipes, one for everyday use, a plain Billiard. The Billiard features a cylindrical bowl with slightly convex flanks and a round shank approximately as long as the bowl is high.

In more generally accepted terms, the Billiard meets that criteria more loosely and can feature any stem type and less exacting bowl proportions while still remaining a Billiard. Variants include the Lumberman, Lovat, Canadian, and Liverpool, which all feature elongated shanks of varying configurations, as well as the Stack/Chimney whose bowl is notably taller. In classic Billiards, the forward part of the rim is slightly lower than the back, providing a slightly canted appearance. Billiards are not easy to make correctly. Collectors often judge the acumen of a carver by how well they can render a traditional Billiard. Chamberlain's was just a classic, not very expensive, Billiard.

His other pipe had been a gift from his father, now retired, when he had been at Cambridge University. It was an Oom Paul. The Oom Paul (Afrikaans for "Uncle Paul") is a pipe shape named after Paul Kruger, President of the ZAR (Zuid-Afrikaansche Republiek) during the late 1800s. It's defined as a fully (or at least very deeply) bent

THE WOODLAND PATH MURDERS

shape, typically with a cylindrical, Billiard-like bowl and a nearly vertically upturned shank. Generally, the Oom Paul is noted for being comfortably clenched while also offering a deep bowl with plenty of tobacco capacity. The shape is also sometimes called a Hungarian.

He didn't use it much these days as he felt it made him look a little ostentatious. He didn't have a deer stalker hat either so he usually smoked it in private, at home mostly, for nostalgia's sake.

He lived in a victorian terraced town house that was on 3 floors above ground with a lower ground floor converted into a flat where his housekeeper Mrs Frobisher lived. She had been widowed in her 50s with no immediate family and seemed happy to take care of Chamberlain's house and domestic duties.

The rest of the house had 3 good size bedrooms on the upper floors and 2 reception rooms and kitchen on the ground floor. The dining room was really used as his study. It was an old fashioned interior but clean and tidy thanks to Mrs Frobisher.

At 41 years old, he was of slim build, 5'11" and still with his own hair, including a moustache he had grown the previous year in support of Movember and had kept, as he thought it added gravitas to the pipe smoking. Ralph Chamberlain was in pretty good shape. He wasn't a fitness nut but did exercise as much as he could. Walking was his main love, whether that be through the streets of a built up town or city or the open countryside, it didn't much matter to him. There were things to observe in both situations. He liked to observe people as much as places.

People watching was an art. You had to be careful that the people you were watching were not aware of it as they might think it was creepy and you were some kind of weirdo. Chamberlain found it useful for his work, learning how people reacted in different situations and to a variety of other people. Friends, lovers, work colleagues, enemies. They all had different aspects to the human condition. Useful when dealing with criminals and potential witnesses.

He also loved fishing, though didn't have much time for it these days.

Closing the front door he walked down the 4 steps to the pavement and got into his car, a 7 year old Vauxhall Cavalier. It wasn't flashy but comfortable and so far reliable, touch wood, he thought as he pulled out into the road.

The journey was fairly painless and he got to the Supermarket in just over 20 minutes. As he walked round the aisles, he thought about going back into work the next morning. He would probably be late in, he usually was, if he was going to the station at all, but it meant his team would have time to settle down and get ready for the day and whatever that would hold. No doubt he would have a fair amount to catch up on after his holiday, not least a mountain of paperwork. He hoped there were no major incidents to deal with, not just yet anyway. His mind was still with the sunshine of Spain.

He took a leisurely journey around the

supermarket. There was no particular hurry this evening. He should buy healthy food. He wasn't an idiot, he knew what was good for him and what wasn't. It was never as easy as that though was it? Living on his own meant catering was difficult to manage. If he bought a load of healthy fresh food, quite a lot of it would go off before he got the chance to use it. He didn't like wastage. Ready meals were convenient, particularly during the week when time was of the essence.

He might cook something properly at weekends, if he wasn't wrapped up in a case. There were no set hours really for a CID detective. Criminals didn't work to set hours so nor could he.

Sometimes his housekeeper would leave a proper hot meal in the oven for him but there had been some close calls when he hadn't arrived home as early as he had hoped and the said meal was blackened and ruined. Potential for burning the house down.

Compromise. He bought some ready meals but also quite a lot of fresh fruit....and some wine of course. He wasn't a heavy drinker but there were times when a glass of two, combined with his pipe, made for a very relaxing evening.

At the till he recognised the look from the cashier that said 'your a single loner then' whilst scanning his goods. You had to pack your own bags these days, and pay for them. If he ever remembered to bring some of the bags he had collected over the years he would save the planet single handed....well, free a whole draw at least.

He loaded the shopping in the boot of the car and headed back towards home. As he was driving he reflected on how much he loved his home ton of Warwick.

It was big enough to be called a town and have its' own police station and CID department, despite being quite near to bigger places like Coventry and Birmingham. He guessed that their CID tests were busy enough in the cities without having to worry about his little town. Suited him, for sure.

He got home, unloaded the shopping and chucked a ready meal in the microwave. He could remember when microwave ovens first became popular. Certain factions got hysterical about the dangers of leaking radiation and wouldn't go near them. He wasn't aware of anyone who had suffered from the use of such an appliance and he reckoned nearly every kitchen in the country probably had one. Air fryers was the latest craze, He hadn't succumbed to them yet.

He ate his meal, beef lasagne, accompanied by a generous glass of Merlot. Afterwards, he settled into his comfortable armchair. Time for the pipe to come out. The room slowly filled with a bluish haze. He fell asleep, pipe resting precariously on his knee.

He had a very vivid but odd dream. In the way of some dreams, the landscape was slightly surreal but he couldn't put his finger on what was different to normal. It didn't really matter. He was an architect, working on a huge project which had to be finished by the weekend.

If he failed to finish it in time, the criminal he was chasing would get away scot free. This was slightly confusing as one minute he seemed to be working on architectural drawings, the next he was poring over forensic evidence and witness statements.

Then he was chasing someone through a half built construction, never quite seeing, let alone catching the shadowy criminal. The building itself was huge, some gothic, some Tudor features with beams, some modern with large expanses of glass. Then the building was on fire. He felt the heat.

Then his ex-girlfriend was pleading with him to take her back. It was slightly bewildering because he couldn't quite recognise her. She started to take her clothes off....

He awoke with a jolt to find that an ember from his pipe had fallen onto his leg and burnt through the material. It singed his leg and he swore.

For some reason the main thing he remembered from his dream was the worry about the criminal getting away scot free. A phrase he had used and heard many times but wasn't sure of the derivation. He googled it on his phone and it turned out to be a medieval form of tax evasion, a scot being a unit of tax, so if you avoided paying the tax you got off 'scot free'.

The rest of the dream began to fade in detail, despite having been so vivid. He vowed to write more of his dreams down as soon as he woke up. He probably wouldn't though.

He took himself off to bed. It wasn't that late, although the dream had seemed to go on for ages, he clearly hadn't been asleep very long.

# CHAPTER 3

There was no doubt in his mind that they would both now have to die. It was the only logical outcome. He felt nothing towards the second victim, just the slight inconvenience of the situation.

It was time for him to move. His dark clothing should avoid him being noticed as he stalked his prey….both of them.

It was difficult to be completely silent moving through the leaf and twig strewn woods but there was a fairly gusty wind blowing which helped to disguise any sounds he made. This had in fact formed part of his planning, checking the weather forecast and choosing the night that the winds were predicted. Oh yes, every little detail was important.

He crept right to the edge of the woods. The two prey victims were making their separate ways along the opposite edge of the same field. It was delicious. Main victim was unaware of prime hunter and secondary hunter who was unaware of prime hunter, who was aware of both prey. He couldn't have made this up, well, not all of it.

This was a fluid, dynamic situation and he would have to use all his skill to pull this off without any hitches. He didn't like hitches, they got in the way and also made it more likely he would get caught. He didn't want to get caught, though it would probably happen one day. He wondered if his nemesis Inspector Chamberlain would be assigned this case once the gruesome enactment had been discovered. He hoped so. It was part of the grand plan.

Now, should he go straight across the field or work his way round the edge, and if the latter, should he go clockwise or anticlockwise? One would put him in front of the main prey, the other would place him behind both victims. If he could go unseen the best choice was to go straight across as this would leave open more options.

Straight across it was then. Hopefully the other two protagonists in this were too busy concentrating on their own missions to notice him. He set off carefully. The field had been left to grass, presumably to be cut for winter feed at some point. It was only a couple of inches high at this point but made a great surface for stealth walking. The rabbits probably loved it too, hence the presence of the main victim. Half way across the field he stopped dead in his tracks. He had noticed a soft dew on the surface of the field. It would leave footprints after his passing through. Damn, he thought. This was not in the plan. Anyone investigating the crime scene would notice his steps across from the other side of the field. What could he do? He was committed.

Then he saw in the corner of the field to his left, some shadowy shapes, and the distant faint sound of munching. Cows. Brilliant. By morning they would have trampled all over the field obliterating his own marks. Problem solved. He might have to help them on their way if they were too settled in the corner.

He moved on slowly, crouching slightly as he went. Victim number one appeared to have stopped at the edge of the field where there was a slight bank in which there were numerous rabbit holes. He was concentrating of setting his snares. Hunter 2/ Victim 2 was creeping up towards him and focusing on his target rather than anything else. He had some distance to go yet though.

He paused for a while, watching the two subjects of his project. The timid one, the now poacher, was fiddling about with his snares and getting ready to set them in the entrances to the rabbit holes. The brash one appeared to be just watching Timid for the time being.

Should he move now, thought the hunter? He couldn't wait all night. He was starting to feel a bit of a chill and the dew was beginning to soak through his clothing. *Ok, let's get this over and done with* he told himself.

As he approached these two, both unaware of what was about to happen, he smiled again. What a great night this was turning out to be.

# CHAPTER 4

Detective Inspector Ralph Chamberlain sat behind his desk in his corner office. He had a fresh cup of coffee before him and he was waiting for his team to bring him up to date on what had been going on in his absence. Very little he hoped. Going on holiday was actually quite arduous.

You spent the two weeks before the holiday making sure you were caught up with everything and had handed over any open cases to whoever was going to cover for you. You went on holiday, the time which seems to fly by faster than at any other time. Then, on your return you had to catch up with all that had happened while you had been away. This usually involved a mountain of paperwork as well.

Warwickshire Police is the territorial police force responsible for policing Warwickshire in England. It is the second smallest territorial police force in England and Wales after the City of London Police. It has been through many amalgamations with other forces in the area including Coventry and West Mercia. Now, though, it has returned to being its' own proud force.

There are only 15 or so Police Stations in

the territory. Warwick Police have an administrative building in Priory Road, at a junction known as Northgate, where The Criminal Investigation Department are based.

It is a Georgian building on 3 floors, made out of local limestone. Chamberlain's office was on the first floor of the building, overlooking the carpark. Not very picturesque but handy if you were looking out for the arrival of top brass and wanted some warning.

He actually spent as little time as possible in his office, preferring to be out and about, pipe in mouth, going through a case in his head. The office had distractions, like that mountain of paperwork, and people knocking on his door. Very distracting.

However, this morning he needed to catch up and the best place for doing that was the office. He wondered idly who would be the first to arrive. He had his suspicions. He would put money on it being his Detective Sergeant.

DS Tom Harris had been working with him for about 3 years now. Very competitive, he liked to be first to arrive at meetings and first at a crime scene if possible.

"Morning Tom" he said as his prediction came true and DS Harris walked through the open door.

"Morning Sir. How was Barcelona?" said Harris.

Chamberlain mused that this was protocol when someone had been away on holiday but suspected Harris was not really interested so he kept the response short.

"Splendid thank you Tom". He would quite like to have someone he could relay his experiences to. Someone who had a genuine interest. Oh well. Maybe Mrs Frobisher, his housekeeper, might lend an ear.

"Excellent" said Harris.

"Are the others far behind you?"

"Just getting coffees I think Sir" said Harris.

Just as he said this, two more people entered the room. Both Detective Constables, both recently having joined Chamberlain's team.

"Come in, sit down, and let's get on with it" said Chamberlain.

They spent the next 45 minutes going over the things that had been ongoing when the Inspector had left and the things that had happened in his absence. It was all pretty mind numbing stuff and Chamberlain found his mind starting to wander a little. Where would he go on his next adventure? Budapest maybe....

"Sir?" Said Harris, pushing through Chamberlain's thoughts of foreign cities.

"What?"

"I said, that seems to be it for the moment Sir".

Said Harris.

"Good. Good. Let me know if you need me for any of those follow ups." He said.

"Will do Sir" said Harris.

Chamberlain realised he had been fiddling with his pipe in his pocket and decided he needed to go outside for a smoke.

"Just going to pop out the back for a smoke" he said.

They had all left his office already and probably didn't hear him. He got up, walked out of his office and through the open plan area where his team had their desks. He was just starting to go down the stairs, anticipating the relaxing smoke he was about to enjoy when there came a shout from behind him.

"Sir, two bodies have just been found" It was his DS. *Blast it, nearly got away.*

# CHAPTER 5

The psychopath was reliving his handy work. It pretty much went to the revised plan. A little more blood than he had hoped for but all in all he was happy. Two dead and he had made it look like they had killed each other. Victim one had a large knife protruding from his chest and victim 2/hunter 2 had one of the poacher's snares tight around his neck, the fingers of both hands bloody from trying to remove it, in vain. It's hard enough to remove a snare once it has tightened but with someone pulling on it from behind and driving the attached ground peg into your shoulder, it is impossible.

He had positioned the bodies so that it looked like the prime victim had had time to whip the snare over the other man's head and draw it tight before succumbing to the fatal stab wound in his chest. This knife had the finger prints of the second man on it, very obvious in the blood that soaked the handle. Whilst wrapping the dead fingers around it, he had made sure his own prints were not there.

He positioned the other body as if the victim had stumbled a little way away from the fight scene before running out of air, and life itself.

Actually what had happened was that the psychopath had opted to go to the left, creep up on the prime victim and stab him soundly in the chest. He then waited for the second man to arrive on the scene only to find the dead body of the man he was stalking.

As predicted, he had stooped down to check the body, whereupon the prime hunter had crept up behind him from the shadows where he was waiting. It had been easy to slip the snare he had taken from the first dead mans bag over his head and pull tight.

He had watched in fascination as the second man had flailed around desperately trying to save his own life. This had gone on for a few minutes until at last there was no more movement and only silence.

He didn't know what the relationship had been between the two men. It didn't much matter to him. His prime victim was dead and now he had a bonus kill as well. This would make a tricky conundrum for Inspector Chamberlain if he was assigned the case.

The next part of the plan would make sure this happened.

He had cast around in the semi light to make sure he had left nothing of his own at the scene. As he was leaving he heard a noise to his left. It would appear that one of the snares set by the first man had had success and a rabbit was caught in the last throws of life. He watched it for a while. He felt no animosity to the rabbit but he didn't have time or inclination to save it. He left the scene.

Just to finish off he went over to where the cows were huddled and he shooed them out into the middle of the field and all over his footprints. That should do it.

He'd worked methodically and silently with no fear of discovery. His victims had come to the chosen area as prompted by him, not wanting to be discovered poaching themselves. The field lay between two pieces of woodland at least half a mile from any dwellings or main roads.

Thinking back over his activities, he was proud of himself. He had had to adapt and change on the fly. Quick decision making. He was good at this. Time to relax a bit and wallow in the self-congratulation. He had no one to share his victory with so he had to clap himself on the back, metaphorically speaking.

# CHAPTER 6

Chamberlain went back into the crew room. The psychopath had no need to worry about him being assigned to the case. He had the most experience currently at this station. His immediate boss, DCI Rebecca Flemming relied on his wide experience, both in Warwick and previously in Bristol.

"OK what have we got" said the Inspector.

DC Norrish stood up from behind his computer monitor.

"Apparently a farmer out along the old Birmingham Road found his cattle a bit skittish when he went to bring them in for milking first thing this morning." He paused, looking down at the print out he held in his hand.

"He had a look around the field and noticed something just inside the tree line along one side of the field. On closer inspection he saw it was a body. He rang it in straight away and the local bobbies went out to the scene."

"Ok, what did they find and are they still out

there?" Said Chamberlain.

DC Norrish cleared his throat and read on.

"They apparently approached the scene along a little used path through the woods. When they got there they confirmed the body of a man. On looking around the area they found the second body. They said that the ground looks very churned up as if there was a fight…. Oh, and yes they are still out there".

" Ok, Tom you're with me. Let's get out there." Chamberlain's pipe smoking would have to wait for a little longer.

"Norrish and err…"

"It's DC Louise Dixon" said the other DC. She looked very young to Chamberlain. She had only joined the team 2 weeks before he had gone on holiday so he didn't know her very well yet.

"Yes, quite. Well you two had better set up the incident room and get things ready for us when we get back. Ok?"

"No problem sir" said DC Adam Norrish. He had been with the team for a couple of years now and knew the drill. Get the large smart screen hooked up and running, connected to the internal network, ready for Chamberlain when he got back. Also, get the tech boys to make sure they had decent internet access and printers primed with paper and ink. Norrish was 26, about 5'10, skinny and had close cropped hair. He was single at the moment and wasn't in a hurry to change that. He wanted to concentrate on his career in the police force. He saw Chamberlain and Harris as his mentors. They were what he wanted to be, eventually, but he knew he had a lot to learn before he got that far and he didn't want the distraction of being involved with a girl. Sure, he would flirt on a night out and maybe steal a kiss if the opportunity came along but that was it, for now.

Chamberlain and Harris hurried out of the room and headed for the car park. Chamberlain was not a good passenger so despite the protocol, he was going to drive. DS Harris was used to this.

As they drove along the road out of Warwick, DS Harris asked his boss "Sir, have you ever heard of a fight where both sides end up dead?"

"No I haven't lad but let's not jump to any conclusions. We haven't even arrived on scene yet" replied Chamberlain. "You know what I always say at the beginning of a case".

"Keep and open mind and follow the evidence?" asked Harris, knowing full well the answer.

"Don't let your imagination run away with you either. Having said that, no I haven't come across such a scenario before."

Privately, he thought about the old custom of duelling with pistols and maybe if both parties got off a lucky shot then maybe they would both die. But this wasn't like that at all.

They drove on towards their destination in silence for a while, both thinking about this and the likelihood of such an outcome. It was true, anything was possible and sometimes you just couldn't make these things up. It was an interesting angle to look at and investigate but they shouldn't ignore other evidence with the risk of going down the wrong path.

They neared their destination as described to them by DC Norrish and could see a marked Police Car parked in a lay-by presumably near to the crime scene. They pulled up behind it and waited for the uniformed officer to approach them. There was a mutual recognition as they had worked on cases before. No need for an ID check.

"Hello Sir. I wondered if you would be given this one. Access is not that easy. There is a path through the woods which doesn't look as if it has been used much recently. The crime scene is about half a mile up into the woods."

"Ok thanks Bob. Do we need wellies?"

"No you should be fine Sir" said the officer.

The two CID detectives got out of the car and made their way to the start of the footpath. The uniformed officer was not wrong. The entrance to the path was not that obvious and there appeared to be no signage.

They set off walking through the woods

towards the crime scene, being careful to look for any clues as to who else may have been up the path recently. Footprints being the obvious one but of course they didn't know how many police or SOCOs had been up there before them. That would be a tricky task to eliminate them to see if there were any that could be either one of their victims, or anyone else for that matter.

As they approached the crime scene they saw the usual trappings including police tape cordoning off what looked like quite a large area. Unusually there were two tents erected over what they assumed were the bodies of the two deceased.

"Who do you think we've got?" said Tom

"What, Forensics or Pathology?" asked Chamberlain

"Well, both really Sir" answered Tom.

DI Ralph Chamberlain was fiddling with his pipe in his pocket, an un-holed one thus far, but he daren't light up, even in the open air, for fear of the wrath of the SOCO team.

"DI Chamberlain I presume" said a voice from behind a surgical mask, mimicking the supposed greeting of Henry Stanley to Dr. Livingstone in deepest darkest Africa in 1871. It did feel somewhat remote where they were in the woods. It was hard to see who it was as they were covered in crime scene protective gear from head to toe. He did, however, recognise the voice.

"Indeed," said Chamberlain, then played along with the quip. "I am glad I found you in this jungle Richard."

Richard Bewley was the senior local Crime Scene Investigator, and Chamberlain had worked with him many times before. They had a good relationship so he was relieved to find him at the scene. He was very good at his job, if slightly reliant on whimsical greetings and phrases. A cliche, but probably a coping mechanism for the grim sites he had to deal with in his chosen career.

"I know it's early days Richard, but anything to report so far?" asked Chamberlain.

"You know me, never one to jump to conclusions, like yourself Ralph" replied Bewley. "Though I would say this is an intriguing one. Trying to work out who died first is going to be fun. I suppose that will be important for you and your lot" he continued.

Chamberlain gazed around the scene for a few moments then asked "Any indications that there could be other parties involved?"

"Ooh, I like your way of thinking. Nothing obvious but I will bear it in mind and no doubt the autopsies will give an idea in due course. You'll have to wait for the SOCOs to establish if there are signs of third parties around the scene. I'll get on with it then"

Bewley turned back to the job in hand.

"Tom" said Chamberlain."can you speak to the SOCOs and see if they have any preliminary findings? I am going to have a wander."

DS Harris was used to his boss's foibles "Of course Sir" he replied, fishing out his notebook as he walked away.

DI Chamberlain let out a big sigh. *Here we go again* he thought to himself.

"I'll meet you back at the car in about 30 mins" he shouted after his DS. Said Sergeant raised an arm in acknowledgement.

He wanted to get a panoramic view of the scene from a distance so he went to the edge of the woods and stepped into the field. He looked around cautiously. Cows had been mentioned and whilst not inherently dangerous, it depended on whether they had calves with them, or even a bull.

He could see a small group of them in the opposite corner of the field and they seemed calm enough with no offspring or servicing bull with them.

He fetched into his pocket for his pipe and began to fill the bowl with the flake once he had teased it out of the tin into a burnable bolus. He puffed away at it until there was a glow from the bowl and a bit of a fug of smoke hanging around him. He didn't move for a while, just taking in the scene around him. *What had happened here* he thought to himself. Cows. Important or not? He'd come back to that. For now they needed to identify the victims and notify any relatives. Get the ball rolling on the investigation. What a great welcome back from his holiday. Hey ho!

He walked the length of the field and back again, puffing on his pipe and enjoying the taste and the slight buzz of nicotine. Nothing obvious occurred to him so he crossed back to the woods and headed back to the car. Harris was waiting there, patiently, chewing on his pen.

"Right, Tom. Back to the ranch ... and don't spare the horses."

They would have to try to find witnesses and relatives. Informing people they had lost a loved one was a painful but necessary duty. There was no easy way to do. Best not to beat around the bush, just come out with it.

There might not be many witnesses, if any, but friends and colleagues should be spoken to. Chamberlain hated the way witnesses on cop programs always seemed to hate the police. In his experience, most witnesses weren't hostile, if they were innocent. They were generally helpful, as much as they could be. If they were guilty of something or were trying protect someone, that could be a different matter altogether.

# CHAPTER 7

The psychopath was long gone from the scene of his exploits. On leaving the macabre theatre in the woods he hadn't returned across the field, the way he had come. He had followed the path deeper into the woods away from the road. There were about 300 acres or so of mixed, mostly native deciduous trees and the path led all the way through to more farmland on the other side and a small back road that would lead him to where he had parked his car earlier that evening. Nobody would see him. No witnesses.

By the time he got back to his flat it was the early hours of the morning. He was very pleased with himself. *Somebody had to be pleased with him* he thought to himself.

On this occasion (he had killed before) he had no need to dispose of any murder weapon. The victims had provided their own. Very thoughtful. He would have to do something with his clothing and footwear but no immediate rush for that. The police couldn't possibly be that close on his heals.

In fact, the next part of his carefully worked out plan was to give them a little nudge. More specifically, a nudge to Detective Inspector Ralph

Chamberlain. He would have to be careful and not rush this part of the plan. He wasn't a very patient man so it could be difficult to control himself.

He needed something to distract him for the time being. Another project? Tempting but possibly a little too distracting. A hobby? As a child his hobby had been tormenting animals but this had now lost its' attraction. Now he had killed one of his own kind nothing else would do.

He sat in his armchair and relived the previous night again, in delicious detail in his mind. The way neither victim had no idea of his presence until it was too late, for both of them. The look of utter surprise, turning to terror, when they realised he was going to kill them.

There had been very little noise throughout the whole event. Just a bit of gurgling really, and gasping for final breaths. There was a strange moment where the two victims had appeared to be looking at each other in a way that suggested they knew one another and were trying to work out what the hell was going on. Maybe they did, It didn't matter now anyway.

He thought back to how he had chosen his victim, victim 1 in fact. Victim 2 had been forced upon him. Circumstances initially beyond his control but a problem that he had quickly overcome and of which he had easily gained control.

It had been in the pub that he had first seen his prey. He had sat quietly at the end of the bar, nursing and gently sipping his whisky & soda.

There had been a small group of what he had

assumed were farm labourers or the like, enjoying a pint or two after a hard physical days work. A couple them were loud and got louder as the pints went down. But one in particular seemed a little quiet and shy and dare he say vulnerable. Perfect.

Over the next few weeks he'd taken up his position at the end of the bar at the same time of the day, early evening in fact. Like clockwork, the group of workers would come in and start the daily ritual of post work drinking. It wasn't always the same bunch but his 'subject' was usually there.

He would surreptitiously study the group, though mainly the one of his focus was the timid one. After a few nights of this he overheard the conversation turn to night time activities by which was meant poaching trips out on remote farmland.

One of the brash ones turned to the timid one and said "Hey, you like to pot a rabbit or two don't you mate?"

"Yeah, s'pose." said Timid.

"Where do you go 'round 'ere then? My misses would love some free meat for the table." said Brash.

Timid didn't look happy about the line of questioning. Poachers were very protective about good hunting grounds. *Lazy bugger can find out for himself* he thought inwardly.

Out loud he said "Well it varies to be honest and I'm looking for a new spot at the moment." With more bravado than he felt inside.

Brash muttered something under his breath and didn't look happy.

The man at the bar noted all of this and decided to make a suggestion to Timid. The conversation of the group changed and soon the men were finishing up their drinks and heading home for their tea.

He had caught Timid's eye and beckoned him over. The poacher came over nervously.

"I know a good place mate, if you are interested" said the stranger.

He had described in detail how to find the spot, somewhere he knew very few people went and was teeming with rabbits.

Thinking back now, he should have paid more attention to Brash over those few weeks, and seen the growing friction between the two. Sloppy. It wouldn't happen again.

He got up from the armchair and went to stand in front of his large mirror. He stood there for some time looking at himself. What would be his next move? His next plan. His next victim. Slowly, a smile appeared on his face. He knew.

# CHAPTER 8

Back at the station the team were waiting for their DI to come in and ask for updates on the progress of the investigation. Because of the complexities they had drafted in some more help from Uniform.

Harris and Chamberlain arrived back at the station.

"You go up and start the ball rolling will you Tom? Said the DI.

"Sure, no problem" said Harris

He knew his boss wasn't really keen on the briefings in the incident room. His DS could update him with all the facts they collected and other developments. He would go in, of course, if anything major happened but it looked like this was going to be an open and shut case with no other parties involved.

"Let me know as soon as you have confirmed IDs and any other forensics. It will be a while before the result of the autopsies." said the DI.

"Will do Boss" answered Harris.

Chamberlain parked up, they both got out and Harris headed for the building. Chamberlain headed out of the car park and into the street. He needed to think. The pipe came out again. He began to walk, in no particular direction.

*Open and shut, right? Cows.*

After about 20 minutes he found himself down by the River Avon that flowed through the town. Did all towns have a river running through them he wondered. Probably. They were where most civilisations congregated for the purposes of communication and food. By rivers or by the sea. Good for defence in some circumstances as well, he guessed.

He loved fishing when he had the time. His father had taught him. Fly fishing mostly. Trout, and the occasional salmon or sea trout. He could see his father now, standing patiently in his waders, mid steam, working the fly and tempting the hidden prey. He had smoked a pipe as well. Kept the midges away he used to say.

He had fished for small fish in the canal where his grandparents had lived, using a cheap rod, small hook and rolled up bits of bread with a float secured to the line. He would sit for hours waiting for the float to go under so he could strike. He caught a few small perch and nothing more.

When he was a bit older his father had taught him to fly fish. Firstly in a large park with short grass.

He gave him a nine foot fly rod and showed him how to cast, with no fly on to begin with, thus avoiding catching his own ear or worse, an eye.

He got quite good at this and his father arranged to take a trip to Scotland where they could fish for Salmon and Sea Trout. This had been a real adventure for him. It wasn't just about the fishing, it was spending time with his father. The smell of pipe smoke mixed in with midge repellant and wax oil for his father's waterproof jacket.

He did catch fish but seemed to spend most of the time sorting out tangled lines or tying on a new fly, having lost the one he was fishing with high up in a tree behind him.

His mind went back to the two victims. It appeared that at least one of them was snaring for rabbits. Poaching really, but no-one really bothered about it as wild rabbits could be a bit of a pest. As long as people didn't damage the land….or get into fights and die. Very inconvenient.

Just then his dratted mobile rang in his pocket. He fished it out. Harris. He pushed the accept button.

"Yes Harris? He barked.

"Er, you said to let you know when we had anything boss." Said the DS nervously.

"Yes, sorry Tom. Go ahead" placated Chamberlain.

"We have both IDs now sir. The stabbed victim is Ronald Denton and the garrotted one is Charles

Foxborough. Both locals. Uniform are on their way round to their addresses to find next of kin." Said Harris.

"Are either of them known to us Tom?" asked the DI.

"Denton has been had up for poaching but was let off as the landowner didn't press charges. Foxborough is clean" informed Harris.

"Ok, thanks for that" said Chamberlain.

"One more thing sir. They both had receipts in their wallets from the Bell & Tankard pub in the High St." Harris added.

The call ended. A trip to the pub then. Chamberlain left the serenity of the river and headed up into the bustle of the town. The pub was not far away, he knew it vaguely. Not his type of establishment. He preferred a quiet Country Pub rather than a busy town pub.

Warwick, the County town of Warwickshire, which lies just south of Birmingham, is full of architectural gems of England's mediaeval history. It is one of the reasons that Chamberlain was so keen to get back to the town at the first opportunity. It may also have sparked his interest in history and architecture. Many buildings reflected the history of medieval architecture. The Priory, the Hospital and not least the Castle, founded by William The Conqueror.

The pub in question was in fact of Tudor origin but it was thought that it was built on the site of an original ale house. Of course, they played the haunted card and it being the favourite pub of some historical figure, Chamberlain forgot which one.

Walking up from the river he reflected on how many thousands, no, millions of people must have walked on these same roads and pathways over the centuries. Visitors not only from within the British Isles but from all over the world.

In true European spirit, Warwick is formally twinned with Saumur in France and Verden in Germany. It also has friendship ties with Havelburg in Germany and Formigine in Italy. Chamberlain was still not entirely sure of the purpose of twinning, other than a good excuse for a jolly for the town's officials, but he was prepared to accept there were probably other benefits, not least tourism, and maybe cultural exchange.

As he walked down Jury Street he could see Warwick Castle off to his left. He had spent many hours as a child exploring the building and grounds. Jury St turned into the High St. He walked past the Lord Leycester, timber framed buildings from the 14th century, and then he turned off right, up Bowling Green Street.

Many of the central streets of the town were destroyed by the Great Fire of 1694. The buildings which were burnt, and many which were not, were re-built in the handsome style of the late 17th and early 18th centuries. Some timber framed buildings survived and the Lord Leycester and the Bell & Tankard were among them.

The pub was located in Market St, just down from the Market Hall Museum, a prominent 17th century building exhibiting the history of the town.

Chamberlain put his still burning pipe in his pocket and entered the pub, taking mental note of the layout and the clientele. It was pretty quiet, just a couple of late morning coffee drinkers and one early liquid luncher.

DI Chamberlain walked over to the bar and got the attention of the barman, a portly man probably in his fifties. He was pulling a slightly bluish liquid through one of the real ale pumps, cleaning the lines Chamberlain assumed.

"Morning Sir, what can I get you?" said the barman.

"Morning" replied Chamberlain. "Just a coffee please. Latte"

"No problem, coming right up. Take a seat and I'll bring it over to you."

"Thank you" said Chamberlain, casting round for somewhere suitable to sit. He wanted to ask the barman a few questions and it wasn't too busy so he hoped he would be able to leave the line cleaning for a few minutes.

He sat patiently, thinking about cows and

footpaths. On the surface, it looked like it might be a simple case that they could wrap up and move on from. But then, when had it ever been that easy? *Well, never*, he thought to himself. He couldn't help but be cynical. He was paid to be cynical.

The barman was bringing his coffee to the table he had chosen to sit at. Placing it down, Chamberlain noticed he had managed not to spill any into the saucer. There was also a coffee time biscuit perched on the edge of the saucer, together with a tea spoon.

"Thank you very much" he said.

"Pleasure" said the barman.

"Um, have you got a couple of minutes? I am a DI with the local CID and we are investigating an incident that happened not far from here" explained Chamberlain.

"Err... yeah ok" said the barman, looking around to see if he had any waiting customers. He pulled out a chair and turned it slightly so that he could still see most of the bar. "What's it about then?" He asked.

Chamberlain shifted slightly in his chair and leaned forward slightly.

"We have had two bodies found up in the woods just off the Old Birmingham Road. Both had receipts from here in their wallets. Preliminary findings show the bodies to be those of a Ronald Denton and a Charles Foxborough. Do you recognise the names" asked Chamberlain.

" Oh my god! Yes I know both quite well. Ron and Charley. They are regulars, part of a small group of after work drinkers. You know, 2-3 pints after a long day and then home for their tea." Said the Barman, whose colour had drained making him appear corpse-like himself. "What happened?" he asked.

"Well, it's early days of course. We have only just opened the investigation it would appear that no one else was involved." Chamberlain said, immediately regretting having said even that much. "Please keep that to yourself by the way. Were they good friends then?" He added.

The barman thought for a second or two "I would say Ron and Charley were affable acquaintances rather than good friends, if you know what I mean."

"Can you describe them for me?" Asked Chamberlain. It was always possible that the ID found on the bodies didn't belong to one or both of them. Unlikely of course until formal identification he had to cover all bases.

"Sure. Little Ron was rather timid I would say. Sparky, I think he is…was, rather. He never mentioned a wife or partner. He did like to supplement his table with a few rabbits, or fish from the river. Poaching I guess you would call it." The barman paused as if remembering something. "Yeah, in fact he was talking about it last night. Said he had a new area to try out."

"And this Charley? Was he into the same activity?" Probed Chamberlain.

"I'm not so sure. He was asking Ron about it last night but Ron wanted to keep it to himself. Charley is a bigger bloke, rather brash. Brick layer by trade. Married, two kids, always moaning about home life." The barman appeared to have finished his descriptions.

"What did Charley think about Ron's secretiveness?" Asked Chamberlain.

"He was a bit huffed I think but I didn't see whatever happened next as I had customers to serve." Explained the barman.

"Ok that will do for the moment. I don't want to keep you from your customers. If you think of anything else…." The Barman was already off his feet and heading for the bar.

"Yeah, sure, no problem" he cast back over his shoulder.

DI Chamberlain sat there for a little longer, thinking about the short conversation. Had this Charley been so annoyed with Ron that he had followed him last night and they had had an altercation leading to both their deaths? Seemed a little far fetched. Affable acquaintances the barman had said. Strange phrase. He knew about the cultural and social phenomena that was after work drinkers. Coppers did it too. A hard days work and a pint or two, or three, seemed well deserved. There was enough time before tea would be on the table.

Was an argument over poaching enough to spark such violence. By all accounts it hadn't really been an argument, though the barman did say he had been called away.

Maybe it was a one in a million occurrence and whatever had set the fight off, it had ended in both men dying. He would have to wait for more evidence from the autopsies and forensics gathered from the scene. That wouldn't be until tomorrow now. He may as well go home. He did.

# CHAPTER 9

It was not that he didn't know the difference between right and wrong, he just didn't care. From an early age these concepts are instilled into us at school if not a home. He was aware of them and couldn't pretend otherwise, even to himself. He was aware that doing the right thing is an act that is in accordance with the law, justice, and morality while doing the wrong thing is an act that is not in accordance with morality or the law. A stable society relies on these definitions.

Still he didn't care. No-one had shown him such moral fibre at home, neither his Mother nor his Father. At school he had kept himself to the shadows and was more often than not daydreaming, looking out of the window in his school classrooms.

Oh they could talk about morals and ethics all day long. They meant nothing to him. HE DIDN'T CARE.

That's not to say that he didn't care about anything. He did. He cared about himself. He cared about his meticulous plans, his projects, and he cared about the outcomes.

He also cared about whether his perceived

players in the game did what they were supposed to do. One particular player wasn't. DI Ralph Chamberlain.

The headlines in the local paper read...

*TRAGIC FEUD LEAVES TWO POACHERS DEAD. LOCAL POLICE NOT LOOKING FOR ANYONE ELSE.*

He was furious. He shouldn't be as this was what he had hoped would happen when they found the bodies. He had worked very hard to create this illusion, and very quickly, given that the scenario was thrust upon him at very short notice.

But it didn't sit right with him. He felt cheated. Chamberlain had gone down without a fight. It was only the second day after his project had played out. Well, he would soon change that. He noticed that he was shaking.

He had killed before, of course, but that was a very personal thing. It wasn't sexual, he got that from his regular visits to the red light district in Birmingham. Functional, not emotional.

He pulled himself together. He wasn't going to let the game finish yet but he hadn't expected to have to add to the initial plan in order to hook DI Chamberlain into his machinations.

He lay down on his bed, closed his eyes and began to think. To Plot.

He needed to grab the attention of this bloody policeman. If he could find someone close to him, that would do it. He didn't seem to have any family around here, no wife or girlfriend, no children. *Lonely bastard* he thought to himself.

Then he remembered something.

# CHAPTER 10

DS Tom Harris had become a policeman because he couldn't think of anything else he wanted to do. He held no high moral ground or any huge desire to help people. Well, not at the beginning. These things had developed over time with him as he progressed in his law enforcement career and he experienced the depths of certain people's depravity and disregard for the law.

No, it was more the fact that he was told working for the police would be a secure, reasonably paid job with great benefits and solid pension. He would probably be able to retire early compared to others. So he had taken a punt, applied and got accepted.

It hadn't taken long, not too many hours of plodding the streets, for him to have higher ambitions. He saw the best and the worst of people in society, both criminals and victims. Just because someone's house was burgled didn't mean they were nice people. It was hard to reconcile sometimes. So after a while, he decided he wanted to work for CID and work major crimes. He had been seconded to a major incident and the man in charge had recognised his abilities, and his ambition. He soon became a Detective Constable.

After a few years it was time to take his sergeant's exams. He flew through them and ended up in Warwick serving on the team of one DI Chamberlain. Despite the quirks of the older man, he respected him immensely. They had worked several big cases together and the combination of the two men seemed to work very well.

His private life had been pretty chaotic, until he had met his current partner, Madeleine or Mads as he called her. She had seemed different to most girls he had known. Not self obsessed and looking in a mirror all the time. They had hit it off pretty much straight away and their first official date had been a night at the cinema. Rather old fashioned but cute in a way. They had seen a psychological thriller and afterwards he had spent the rest of the evening telling her how unrealistic the story line and characters were. Nothing like real life or actual police work. She had laughed at him saying it was only a movie.

He had taken the bull by the horns and kissed her gently on the mouth. She hadn't pulled away….the rest was history, as they say.

He was now 31 and they had been together for over two years. They hadn't really discussed the long term but they were now living together in his flat. It had been an easy decision for both of them.

When he walked into the incident room that morning, he was ashen faced and looked stunned and bewildered. He'd been given some news, by Mads.

"You ok Tom?" asked Chamberlain. "You look like shit! Seen a ghost?"

Tom Harris stood there, still for a few moments. "Err...well...I dunno really" he stammered. "Mads is pregnant" he stated simply.

"Wow, that's fantastic Sarge!" shouted DC Dixon.

"Brilliant news Sarge!" echoed DC Norrish

"Congratulations Tom" added Chamberlain. "Don't look so worried, you will make great parents, I'm sure".

"But we aren't married.... I should marry her....we must get married" babbled Harris.

"Whoa there! Calm yourself Tom. There's plenty of time for that, if, that is, in fact, what you both want." Chamberlain tried to calm his sergeant. "Marriage isn't the be all and end all these days. There are plenty of unmarried couples who have children very happy and successfully. Have you discussed it with Madeleine?"

"Err, no not yet. I'll do that tonight" replied Harris.

He had got home the previous evening, called out to his partner and heard no reply. He wasn't that worried as she, being a nurse, worked odd hours as much as he did. He went into the kitchen and grabbed

THE WOODLAND PATH MURDERS

a can of beer from the fridge. Then there came a call from upstairs.

"I'm up here, Tom" shouted Madeleine. "Can you come up?"

He climbed the stairs, still holding the can of beer. She wasn't in the bedroom. Bathroom then. He wondered if she was ok. He walked into the bathroom and saw her sitting on the closed lid of the loo, holding something in her hand. She looked worried.

"What's up, love?" he asked.

She looked up at him and then down at the object in her hand, then back up at him. It hit him.

"Holy shit, is that what I think it is?" Harris said, in alarm.

"Well, yes. That wasn't quite the reaction I was hoping for, Tom" she said meekly.

"Right, no, well….wow. You're pregnant then?" he said, stupidly.

"Yup, that would be it."

"How….no, don't answer that" he stopped himself asking the idiot question.

They both went downstairs and sat on the sofa, holding hands. They talked about the prospect of being parents and agreed that, although it wasn't brilliant timing, it was wonderful, albeit quite shocking, news. It was obviously going to change their lives. They weren't quite sure how things would change as they hadn't thought about it or discussed it before.

# CHAPTER 11

Mrs Frobisher liked working for Ralph Chamberlain. He was no trouble, as the saying goes. He was a respectable senior Detective and clean living, apart from his retched pipe that kept burning holes in his trousers. She had her own flat, albeit in the basement. She could come and go at any time as long as she kept the main parts of the house clean and tidy she could do as she pleased. One thing she got comfort from was the small garden to the back of the property. Her boss was not a gardener so she took it upon herself to tend the small area

If asked, she probably couldn't express in words what it was about gardening that made her feel good. If she knew how, or could be bothered, she could look it up or talk to someone. But she did know it made her relax and afterwards she felt better for it. In modern parlance, it helped her well-being.

Maybe it was the fresh air or the exercise or just the shear joy of watching things grow. She didn't think she was a neat freak but she did like to see things in a bit of order. It made her good at the gardening, and her proper job of keeping house for DI Chamberlain.

When she lost her husband, Frank, several years ago now, she was lost. She didn't know what to do. They had not been blessed with children and there were no close relatives on either side of the family. She lived in a bit of a trance for a couple of years. Then she saw an ad in the window of a local shop, looking for a live in Housekeeper.

She knew how to keep house, for sure. She could sell her little two-up-two-down and have a nice little nest egg while living in the accommodation provided with the job.

She applied, went to meet DI Chamberlain and he offered her the job, on the spot. They had built a friendly yet professional relationship over the years and she was, if not completely happy, at least content with her lot. She had even joined a local bridge club for her social life.

At the moment she was just sitting in the garden enjoying the fruits of her labour. Nothing much needed doing at the moment. Maybe next week the grass would need cutting again.

She had been reading her book, a classic Jane Austin but now was leaning back in the garden chair and looking up at the clouds. She had read the book before of course but with such a writer, she always found some other nuance when she re-read it. The stories were good. The characters were well formed. She could fantasise about a different life, a different society, a different time. She kept nearly dozing off. Well why shouldn't she? Her work for the day was finished.

She reflected on her life. A simple life, no frills, but she thought she had done ok. Yes, she was widowed but the time she and Frank had had together had made precious memories. He shouldn't have died so young and left her…silly so and so. They had been happy with their lot. A week away in Scarborough every summer. The odd weekend trip to the Dales or the Pennines. They liked to walk together in the hills. Never speaking much, they didn't feel the need.

She'd grown up, a single child, with parents who seemed to talk incessantly. Almost to the point that they couldn't have been listening to what the other was saying as they were talking at the same time. She couldn't see the point. They didn't argue though so that was something. She'd been content as a child, no unrealistic dreams of what she would be when she grew up. She knew she wasn't the brightest spark. Not a dullard either. She just did ok, in all the aspects of her life. It was enough for her.

She'd met her Frank at a local dance. He'd kept looking at her across the dance floor. He clearly wasn't going to pluck up the courage to ask her to dance, so she took the initiative and asked him. The rest, as they say, was history. Then the silly so and so went and died of a heart attack at the age of 56.

She was squinting up at the clouds when she saw something fluttering down out of the sky. It landed about 5 or 6 feet away from her. She couldn't quite see what it was. She got up and walked over to it. It was a glove. A brown leather glove, left hand by the looks of it, with dark staining on it. *How peculiar* she thought to herself. She picked it up and looked around, over the garden fences, to see if there was anyone next door, either side, who might own the lonely glove. Both gardens were empty.

It must have come from farther afield. She would ask neighbours up and down the road. Maybe they had thrown it in a fit of gardeners frustration. It reminded her of a scene from a film she had seen but she couldn't quite remember which one. She put it on a shelf just inside the back door. She would deal with it later.

# CHAPTER 12

Another thing about the psychopath is that he is not a forgiving sort of person. If he felt wronged he always wanted retribution. He felt wronged. DI Chamberlain was dismissing his handiwork and presumably moving on to what he thought were more interesting cases.

He needed to nudge the Inspector, hence the glove which he had kept as a sort of trophy but had now skilfully thrown into the Inspector's back garden. He wondered how long it would take for him to make the connection. He hadn't known the woman would be there in the garden. He didn't think Chamberlain had a wife or partner. No matter, it would expedite the discovery of the glove so no harm no foul.

He thought back to the reason he needed Chamberlain to engage with the game. He wondered if he would remember that far back. Well, he was going to remind him, big time.

Was it really ten years ago? He had been a young man then and Chamberlain a beat cop, early in his career. You could say that the psychopath had been early in his career as well. He hadn't killed at that point...well, not humans at any rate. He hadn't counted the number of animals he had tortured and killed as a boy. He hadn't been fussy, neighbourhood cats, pet rabbits as well as wildlife if he could get his hands on them. He had shot a few birds with an air rifle but that had been too remote, not thrilling enough.

Chamberlain had interrupted what was going to be his first human kill.

PC Chamberlain was nearby on his rounds and rushed over towards the commotion. The killer had to abandon that project and make his escape. Chamberlain had been hailed a hero for saving this man's life and his face was plastered over all the local newspapers.

The unforgiving psychopath had vowed to get his own back on this copper. He would bide his time but one day this chicken would come home to roost. He had lost touch with Chamberlains career as he had moved away, no doubt moving up the ladder of promotion and getting experience in other forces around the country. No matter, he would find him one day and battle would commence.

His first successful human prey had been a work colleague. It had been like an itch that he couldn't scratch. He needed to know what it felt like to take a human life. It had been disappointing in a way, after the first few moments of thrill. It had been a quick death, a knife up and under the rib cage and into the heart. He had had to keep going back to where he had disposed of the body to remind himself.

So far, no one had found this first victim. He

liked the feeling of power and control knowing that he knew but others didn't. Not the police, the nearest and dearest, no one.

After a while, just visiting the site had not been enough and he needed to kill again. He needed to hone his craft and develop a fool proof MO. He had used homeless people as his practice victims. No one took much notice when a homeless person disappeared. They assumed they had just moved on to another city. Anyway, he was doing society a favour, wasn't he. He would kill and then drop the body in a canal or river. Sometimes he would transport a body to the coast and drop it in the sea. It didn't much matter if they were discovered and there would be no connection to him.

## Chapter

The next morning, DI Chamberlain rose early. He had woken at just after 4am having been dreaming about cows, and couldn't get back to sleep so had got up, showered and had some early breakfast.

He supposed he should really go in to his office to catch up with his team. He never relished the thought of being in his office or any part of the station for that matter. It stifled him and his thought processes. His immediate boss, DCI Rebecca Flemming, did not share his view on the matter and made her feelings clear whenever she did manage to catch him at his desk.

No, Chamberlain had enough faith in his team

to let them get on with that side of things. The incident room whiteboard, or big screen as it was now, and all the notes about the crime and the victim were all inside his head. They would update him with any developments or changes.

However, today he hoped to get some information first hand from the SOCOs and possibly a prelim report from the autopsies. Neither of these involved him actually going to his own office or desk so that was something. He would simply have to put his head round the door of the incident room and ask Harris to update him over a coffee in the canteen, Then he could go across the road to the morgue where the autopsies would be happening.

He entered the station via the front door and nodded to the desk sergeant who nodded back but as Chamberlain was passing he murmured "She is about this morning Sir!"

Chamberlain nodded at him again. It was well known that he liked to be warned when his boss was about so that he could do his best to avoid her. Not that he particularly disliked her or thought she wasn't good at her job. He just didn't like to get caught up in long conversation about a case or the office or anything really. When he was ready to update her, he would do so.

He paused, turned back and said in a low voice "Can you call up to DS Harris and ask him to meet me at the cafe round the corner please." He didn't wait for a reply but turned on his heals and went back out through the front door, across the car park, out into the road and then walked round the corner towards said cafe. There he waited for Harris to arrive. They had done this many times before so Harris would not be surprised in the least to get the message from the desk sergeant.

He ordered his favourite coffee, a large Latte, and waited. A few minutes later DS Harris came though the door and approached Chamberlain. He looked a little worried.

"Welcome to the satellite war room Tom. Everything ok? You look a little perturbed." Greeted Chamberlain.

Harris sat down opposite Chamberlain and simply put a newspaper down in front of him, open at the inside page. Chamberlain read the headline about the Poachers feud.

"Bugger" he said simply. "Get yourself a drink and put it on my bill Tom".

Harris got up and went to order his drink and then returned to the table.

"That's my fault I suspect" said Chamberlain. "I let slip to the Barman at the pub that we didn't think anyone else was involved with the deaths. I did ask him to keep that to himself but you know what people are like. They have a bit of knowledge they know others don't have and they want to share it, sort of show off their upper hand. Not a great stretch of the imagination to think that it got round the pub quickly and then to the media. They have a nose for this kind of thing".

"Ah, ok. I did wonder how that got out" said Harris.

"Well it is out now, nothing we can do about it until we have more evidence. On that subject, anything for me this morning?" Chamberlain asked.

"Hmm, where to start" said Harris. "Actually, the paper may be right. The SOCOs haven't finished quite yet but they have said that their search of the crime scene did not turn up any evidence of any other parties being involved, and they did search a fairly wide area. Also, no witnesses so far."

"Right. And anything from the morgue? I will go over there once we are finished here but anything you can arm me with before I go?" Asked Chamberlain.

"Again, nothing to indicate anything other than what it appears to be....so far." Added Harris

"Ok well you go back and keep working on the board and let me know if anything else turns up. I'll pop across the road and see our friend the Professor" Chamberlain drank down his coffee and moved to get up.

"You do know we don't use a board any more don't you Sir? We updated to large screens last year" jibed Harris, knowing how much of a technophobe his boss was.

"Whatever" retorted Chamberlain. "Can you arrange to go and talk to that Barman again, I didn't get his details but he's a big bloke, early 50s, messy beard. Read him the riot act and see if anyone else in the pub knew the victims, or saw or heard anything useful."

They both left the cafe, Chamberlain having settled the bill. DS Harris headed back towards the station and DI Chamberlain headed across the road to see Professor Daniel Reed, the man doing the autopsies.

On entering the building he was told that he would have to wait for the Professor who was just finishing up an autopsy and was cleaning up.

While he waited he pondered about his team. Did they object to his frequent absence from the office? His style was probably a little different to most team leaders. The fact that Harris had been with him for a while now and hadn't asked to be moved on must mean something. The other two permanent members, Norrish and Dixon, were quite new so he guessed time would tell on that.

Teamwork was essential, in any environment, but especially in Police work. Chamberlain had done all the courses thrown at him over the yers but nothing could replace the natural formation of a good team. The essentials came naturally - communication, collaboration, trust, and respect.

Each team member has a role to play. All are important to the success of the team. In this way, a team overcomes challenges, solves problems, and achieves goals.

It is also about actively listening to other members of the team. Supporting struggling friends and team mates. Approaching teamwork with a positive attitude.

Maybe he shouldn't worry. His team got results. End of.

A pair of swing doors flew open and a man in green scrubs flew through after them.

"Ralph Chamberlain, welcome to the pleasure dome!" Professor Daniel Reed was known for his inappropriate language.

"Daniel" replied Chamberlain.

"Come through, come through old boy."

Chamberlain followed the Professor back through the double doors and they went into an office just down the corridor. They sat either side of a plain desk with very little on it Chamberlain noticed.

"What can you tell me Professor?" asked Chamberlain.

"Well, although I haven't completed the autopsies entirely, I can tell you a couple of things. Both causes of death are pretty obvious but I guess you were expecting that." The professor paused.

"I'm sensing a 'but' here Professor" commented Chamberlain.

"Yes, very astute of you. I can't tell you which of the victims died first or indeed in what order the attacks happened. That will have to be up to you I'm afraid old boy. On being attacked, either could have responded with fatal effect. The knife wound would not have been fatal immediately, nor the snare garrotte. I also can't say for certain whether or not anyone else was involved. It could be that these two were indeed the instruments of each others deaths." The professor now put his fingers together, as if in prayer, and put them up to his mouth and looked at Chamberlain with raised eyebrows.

"What about tox reports, any drugs or alcohol?" Chamberlain was fishing for anything that could lead to furthering the enquiry.

"Path lab says low alcohol in the blood of both victims but no drugs, or any other suspicious substances. Not surprising if they had been at the pub earlier that evening" said Reed. "They both appeared to be relatively healthy, apart from being dead, of course".

Chamberlain thought for a moment. Could this be an open and shut case after all? Neither forensics nor pathology had, at least so far, revealed anything other than the obvious.

"Has the clothing gone over to forensics yet?"

asked Chamberlain.

"No, still laid out in the preparation room. Would you like a fashion show?" quipped the Professor.

The two men got up and left the sparse office and headed further down the corridor. They got to another, larger room with tables laid out in the centre of the room. On these tables were the two sets of clothing from the respective victims.

"Which is which?" Asked Chamberlain.

"On the left hand table we have the vestments of a Mr. Charles Foxborough who was the garrotte victim and on the right, those of a Mr Ronald Denton, the victim of the knife wound. There is less blood on the former due to the method of the attack" explained Professor Reed.

Chamberlain walked around the tables taking in the last worn clothing of the two victims. Nothing very fancy, or particularly new. He guessed a poacher wouldn't wear his Sunday best on a trip out into the woods at night to catch and kill rabbits. The other set of clothing sat well with the description of a labourer after a days hard work.

"So, to be clear, you are saying that in both cases, the cause of death could have allowed for a reaction from a victim, giving enough time to cause the other's death as well?" queried Chamberlain.

"Yes. A stab wound is certainly not necessarily immediately fatal. I believe the victim bled profusely before he died. He may have had a minute or two in order to launch his attack on the other if the stabbing was the first attack. Similarly, being strangled by a snare would not kill immediately either, so that victim would more than likely have time to stab the other man. One interesting factor is that the wire snare was tightened around the victims neck and then secured by driving the peg at the end of the wire into his shoulder, hence making it almost impossible for the victim to loosen or remove it." Explained Reed.

"Might that suggest that the snare victim was attacked first if the killer had time to drive the peg in?" Asked Chamberlain.

"It's a possibility" agreed Reed.

It was looking like the Newspaper headlines were correct after all. A *Poachers tragic feud* indeed.

"Ok thanks Daniel. I will of course wait for the full autopsy and forensic reports but it looks like a simple open and shut case." Mused Chamberlain.

He was about to leave the room when something struck him. He turned back to the clothing of the stabbing victim and remarked "There is only one glove I see. Do you think that is significant?" He asked Reed.

"Yes, the right hand glove is here but not the

left hand one. The SOCOs may just not have found it, or the poacher may only use the one glove for handling the wire snares, or perhaps a struggling rabbit and its' sharp teeth. Again, I can't answer categorically" said Professor Reed.

On that note, they ended their meeting and Chamberlain headed back outside. He fetched out his pipe and went through the ritual of lighting up, leaving a haze of smoke as he wandered across the road towards the police station.

# CHAPTER 14

The psycho killer was now waiting patiently for Chamberlain to discover the glove and make the connection to his current case. It was a strange feeling now wanting his opponents to catch on to his scheme so that the game could commence properly. Previously he had hidden his escapades well. He was proud of that. After all it was nobody else's business what he got up to in his spare time.

He had quite a lot of spare time at the moment. He was 'in-between jobs' as the saying goes, used mostly by people who are unemployed but don't want to attract the possible stigma attached to that state of affairs. Maybe it was time to up the anti and give DI Chamberlain some more clues as to what was going on. He may not see the glove for some time and even then it may take a while to make the connection.

He decided he would give him a little more time. That would give him the opportunity to develop his scheme down to the most finite detail. In the meantime he needed something to do. Something that wouldn't draw attention to him but something fun.

He fancied spending some time in a really posh

hotel, eating posh and delicious food. For that he would need some more cash. He would do what he normally did when he needed funds. He would take them from someone else. Someone who had plenty and didn't necessarily need or deserve it.

This side adventure would have to happen away from where things were focused at the moment. He didn't want to muddy the waters for DI Chamberlain.

No, he would travel far enough away for it not to come up on the Inspectors radar. He sat in front of his computer and started doing some research.

Nearly an hour and a half later he had his plan and a location. He would travel to Cheltenham and would pay a visit to the world famous race course. Lot's of cash floating around at those places surely? He knew that the government didn't like people having cash as they couldn't keep track of it. Lots of places, including outdoor events, now had the facilities to take card payments with widespread internet access being the norm.

But the gambling fraternity, particularly horse racing, loved their cash. There was something about handing over the readies to a bookie and dreaming of the returns if and when your horse came in.

He had been to race meetings before. He actually liked horses. Something about the power of them being controlled by a relatively small person appealed to his psyche.

He would go tomorrow. He had checked and

there were a few races scheduled for then. If he got there early enough he could spend some time watching the crowds and the bookies and see how the cash flowed round and was dealt with. Bound to be some security and CCTV but he knew how to be careful and minimise his exposure. He would dress in uninteresting clothing so that he didn't stand out from the crowd for a start. Important not to stay in one place for too long, move about slowly and keep to the shadows as much as possible. He was getting excited, this could be fun.

He started to pack up a few essentials for the trip. Small pair of binoculars. Gloves. Notepad and pencil. Wash bag and contents. He would be away for a couple of days. When he got back with his funds, he would decide which hotel to spend a night or two in. He could do that more locally fairly safely he felt.

# CHAPTER 15

DI Chamberlain had taken the plunge and had gone in to the station to address the team in person and to update his DCI. He couldn't put it off and in any case it looked like they were to wrap up this up very quickly. He had phoned DCI Flemming earlier to let her know and give her a brief update. She had seemed relieved that the case was not going to need her involvement. She liked it when her DI was able to cope without her, despite his unconventional approach.

He had grabbed some take out coffees and buns from the cafe, or Satellite War Room, as he referred to it, on his way in. *How kind of me* he thought to himself. They deserved it though.

He entered the incident room and present were DCs Norrish and Dixon, DS Harris and DCI Flemming, all sitting at desks looking expectant.

"Morning all" he said. "Grab a coffee and a bun and let's get on with this. It won't take long by the looks of it."

They all did so obediently, including the DCI. Once settled back at their desks, Chamberlain cleared his throat and leant on the corner of the desk at the from, just in front of the big screen, *where the whiteboard used to be* he thought nostalgically.

He began "Right. Just to recap then. We have two victims and as far as we can tell, no one else involved in their deaths. So far, neither forensics nor pathology have found any evidence of any third parties. It sounds incredible but it looks like they killed each other. At the moment then it looks like case closed. There will be all the reports to collate etc and a report sent to the CPS but if it really is that simple then we will be free to get on with other things." He paused, as if he was afraid someone might say something that would shatter that illusion. They didn't. So he prompted…

"Anyone anything to add? Any new evidence?"

Harris sat forward and spoke "Well, nothing really Sir. I was going to speak to the Barman again but am told he is away for a couple of days. Needed a break apparently. I'll follow up when he gets back just to cross the I's and dot the T's so to speak but other than that no".

It was then DC Dixon's turn. "Both families have been informed and formal idents completed. They were as mystified as every one else and couldn't add any motives or ideas for what happened"

"Ok thank you both" said Chamberlain. He looked over the room with raised eyebrows, slightly titling his head, inviting more comments. None came.

"Right, well tidy up the paperwork and let's move on" wrapped up Chamberlain.

They all got on with their various tasks and Chamberlain decided he would take a walk outside. He had been fiddling with his pipe in his pocket all through the briefing and he needed to scratch that itch.

DCI Flemming stopped him before he got out of the door. "Would you like to do a press conference and let the media know 'case closed?'" she said.

"Errr....well...." Stuttered Chamberlain.

"Don't worry, just kidding, I know what your views are on the media. I'll do it" said Flemming with a slight grin.

"Thank you Ma'm" said Chamberlain. He went out into the carpark and created his usual haze of pipe tobacco smoke.

The rest of the day consisted of filing reports interspersed with smoking and coffee breaks. He felt drained when he got home that evening. He needed some R&R. The house looked clean and tidy, as always. Mrs Frobisher was a gem.

He sat down in his armchair and used the remote to put on some music. He was in his own house so he didn't have to go outside to smoke. He lit the pipe and sat back to enjoy some tunes.

Whereas Colin Dexter's fictitious Detective called Morse liked to listen to certain classical music, Chamberlain's guilty pleasure was prog rock. Seconds Out, the Genesis album recorded live in Paris in 1977 at the Palais Des Sports was one of his favourites. Sacrilege he knew, to some people but he preferred Phil Collins as the lead singer rather than Peter Gabriel. He did also like a bit of Dad Rock, or Cock Rock as one of his friends from school used to call it but tonight was a Genesis night. In his opinion, no one could write complex and richly melodic songs like Genesis did.

As 'Squonk' started to fill the room he sat back and began to relax. A fairly easy return to work after his holiday, he mused. An unusual case he had to admit but you couldn't argue with the evidence, could you?

Then as 'Carpet Crawlers' came on, he started to drift off to sleep, his pipe in his hand resting on his lap. Genesis kept playing.

"Argh, bugger" suddenly he shouted, and brushed furiously at his crotch. A still burning ember had fallen out of his pipe and into his lap. It had burned through the material of his trousers and scalded the inside of his upper thigh.

"Are you ok Mr Chamberlain" came a voice from the hallway. It was Mrs Frobisher. She had come in to check if he needed anything from her before she went out.

"No, no, all good thanks Mrs F" said Chamberlain, feeling like a complete idiot. This burn was not a mendable pocket. These trousers were toast.

"Burnt yourself again have we?" said Mrs Frobisher, popping her head around the door.

Chamberlain turned the music off and beckoned for her to come into the room properly. "Err yes, well, just a bit" he said.

There was a fug in the air from his pipe smoke, mixed with the smell of scorched material. He held his hands in front of himself in an attempt to hide the offending hole in his trousers. He looked like a schoolboy up before the teacher having done something wrong.

"Another hole in the pocket?" asked Mrs Frobisher "I can mend it tomorrow if you leave them out for me but I can't do it tonight I'm afraid as I am going out".

Chamberlain gave a lopsided grin and said "Don't worry. Too far gone this time I'm afraid. There's no saving these trousers! Off anywhere nice?"

"It's bridge night with the girls…oh and I want to call in at the neighbours to ask if anyone has lost a glove. Very strange, one fell into the garden this afternoon while I was having a sit down and a cup of tea" she explained.

"Right…what? Fell into the garden?" Queried Chamberlain.

"Yes, it was very odd actually. A bit like that film with that John Cossack and that Buffy girl and the scene on the ice rink at the end." She said.

"Um, I think you mean John Cusack and Kate Beckinsale, who was in the Van Helsing movies. Serendipity, the film you are talking about I think?" Ventured Chamberlain.

"Yes, yes, that's it" exclaimed Mrs Frobisher. "It seemed to fall out of the sky, just like in that film. I thought one of the neighbours may have flung it in a fit of pique or something"

Chamberlain raised his eyebrows, thinking that might be a possibility but sounded a bit far fetched.

"I've got it here in my bag" she said, pulling out the item in question. "It's not one of mine and I am pretty sure you don't own any gardening gloves".

Chamberlain froze. His heart almost stopped and his stomach seemed to flip. He had seen a glove that looked very much like the match to this one, earlier that day at the autopsy with the clothes from one of the victims.

# CHAPTER 16

Chamberlain had spent a restless evening, and even more restless night, ruminating over the appearance of what appeared to be the other glove belonging to one of his victims. He had carefully taken it off his housekeeper and placed it in an evidence bag (he always carried some in his jacket pocket). It would, of course, be contaminated by the handling by his housekeeper but even so, he needed to preserve any potential evidence.

He had rung DS Harris first thing in the morning and told him to gather the team as early as possible, explaining briefly about the glove. Harris had been a little confused, not being party to the autopsy visit.

Frankly, Chamberlain felt, and looked, like shit when he walked into the incident room.

"Morning" he grumbled, to no one in particular.

"Morning Sir" came a chorus back at him.

"It now seems possible that the case we all but closed yesterday, may not be as simple as we thought. Unless someone is playing silly buggers, we may have a third party or parties involved with this and from what happened yesterday they seem to want to make a game out of this. I am waiting for definite confirmation from forensics but it looks like someone threw the pair to a glove found at the scene, into my garden." Explained Chamberlain.

He looked out at a row of blank faces. His DCI walked into the room at this point and barked "What the hell is going on Chamberlain? I hear that our poachers feud may have turned into something more sinister. Is that right?" She said.

"Well, something hinky is going on, that's for sure" replied Chamberlain.

He sometimes wondered if those higher up the food chain than he was, were more interested in having cases put neatly away rather than actually finding out the inconvenient truths. He guessed it was only human nature to wish for uncomplicated outcomes when you are trying to keep those above you happy and are working to budgets all the time.

"Hinky?" Said the DCI.

Chamberlain had heard the word used on the American police procedural series called NCIS. He liked the word but he didn't want to piss off, or confuse, his superior.

"Sorry Ma'm, something out of kilter has happened. I was going to brief you after this meeting but I see the jungle drums have been working overtime."

He explained again what had happened with the gloves and then fell silent. After a few moments of silence in the room he continued.

"Either someone is being very foolish and is playing a stupid game....or we have a real player who wants to challenge us to find him. If it's the latter, this may not be the end of their game. There may be more deaths." Chamberlain let that sink in for a moment.

"What, you mean we may have a serial killer?" piped up DS Harris.

"Let's not get ahead of ourselves but what is for certain is that we have to re-open this case and dig a lot deeper than we have already." said Chamberlain

Clearly now in even more of a bad mood than when she first came into the incident room, DCI Flemming glared at Chamberlain and said "I did a bloody press conference yesterday afternoon, confirming the poachers feud scenario. Now I'm going to look like a right Charlie! Once you have decided what you are going to do next, I want a full briefing from you Chamberlain". Without waiting for a response she turned and left the room.

"Right. I'm going back to the scene to have another look around. Harris, can you go back to the pub and do a more thorough interview with whoever you can find in there. You can take DC Dixon with you. Norrish, get back to autopsy and forensics and let them know what we are doing and ask them to go over everything again. They won't like it but that's tuff." Said Chamberlain.

He left them to get on with their respective tasks and went to his car. It took him 20 minutes to get to the same lay-by they had parked in a few days previously. He sat in the car for a few minutes trying to order his thoughts. His inner thigh was still sore from the previous days accident. He would leave the pipe where it was for the moment, unlit and in his trouser pocket.

He got out of the car, locked it, and headed up the little used footpath towards the crime scene. This time he was much more alert to his surroundings and walked slowly through the woods, looking down at the path and also to the left and right at the undergrowth. There didn't seem to be anything obvious to him but he would get the SOCO team back up to have a proper look.

Glancing to his left, through the trees, he noticed the cows again. Cows? He wondered what they had seen that night. He also noticed a figure further up the field, possibly the farmer tending his herd. He would try and get to speak to him after he reached the scene of the deaths. It looked now as if this may be a double murder by a third party. Either that or someone was messing with them, for what reason he couldn't fathom at the moment.

Once he got near to the scene he moved over towards the field. He wanted to avoid any further disturbance until it had been re-investigated. Hopefully, as the path seemed little used, no other walkers had been through as yet.

He stepped over the fence, gingerly due to his burn, and hailed the figure on the other side of the field. He got a wave back and they approached each other, meeting somewhere in the middle of the field.

"Morning" greeted Chamberlain.

"'Ow do" responded the man. "You lost? Don't see many folks up through these woods these days."

"Ah, no, no. I am DI Chamberlain and I am involved in investigating the two deaths that occurred here a few days ago. I wondered if I could have a few words. I assume it was you who found the bodies?" He asked.

"Yup, that was me. Very unpleasant. I did give a statement to one of your lot so what else do you want to know" said the farmer.

"Yes, indeed, thank you for that. I just really wanted to ask you about the cows. Would they have been disturbed by a struggle going on in the woods there?" Asked Chamberlain.

"Maybe, depends on how much of a racket was made I s'pose. They would have been fairly bunched together during the night. Cows are herd animals and stick together to reduce the threat from predators, specially at night, not that there are many would take on a cow around here." He explained.

"Right. Do they move around much during the night?" asked Chamberlain

"The majority of lying time occurs overnight. Does vary of course, and they do move around, particularly if spooked" said the farmer.

"Ok, so if something spooked them, they would all move together would they?" Continued Chamberlain.

"Probably" came the reply. "They generally graze around a field facing the same way, again to avoid threats"

DI Chamberlain hadn't been aware that cow behaviour was so ordered or understood but he guessed a farmer would get to know these things from working with them over time.

"Did you notice anything about their demeanour that morning? Were they behaving oddly or seem spooked?" Asked Chamberlain.

"Not really, they settle pretty quick if they are spooked. I did notice one thing. There was a fairly wide path of trodden on dew that seems to go right across the field to the top tree line. Can't really see it now as they have been all over since" said the farmer.

"Right. And do you have much of a problem with poachers in the area?" asked Chamberlain.

"I know it 'appens but to be honest it doesn't

bother me as long as they don't upset the cows or damage the woodland. Rabbits is a pest to us farmers really, so in a way they are doing us a favour" came the reply.

"Ok" said Chamberlain. He could understand the attitude. What harm was little poaching doing to anyone…except the rabbits of course. "Do you mind if I have a wander around the field for a bit? I will try not to disturb the cows."

"Fill ya boots" shrugged the farmer.

They parted company. Chamberlain chuckled at the expression just used by the farmer. He had once looked up the origin of the phrase and apparently English coal miners wore hobnailed boots which were slippery on cobblestone streets, so they carried them home after work so they wouldn't slip. This allowed them to "fill their boots" with coal which would be just enough coal for a family for one day. It was now used as slang for "help yourself" or "be my guest".

Pipe time. Chamberlain lit up and puffed a few times to get the bowl glowing nicely. He set off across the field towards the top tree line, thinking about the responses from the farmer to his questions.

# CHAPTER 17

The killer had a splendid day at the races. He achieved his goal of cash acquisition in a pretty straight forward fashion. No mess. That hadn't been the purpose of the day's exploits.

He had arrived at the racecourse and found a spot in the stands where he could observe what was going on around him and down where the bookies were operating their totes. He spent quite a bit of time watching them and how they took the bets, took the money and secured it in special boxes. This concerned him a little but then he spotted one of the bookies swap the box he had been using for a new one, delivered by a security guard. This guard then removed the full box of money and headed for the admin area.

Ok, so there was his weak point. He started to work out a plan. It would be tricky but then he enjoyed tricky.

He ambled down from the stands and wandered in the direction of the admin block. He walked straight past it, noting there was a 'STAFF ONLY' sign on one of the doors. As he continued he saw a man in normal clothes go in through the door.

He waited a little way away and the same man then came out dressed in a security guard uniform. That was it then. He had to get in there somehow and 'borrow' a uniform.

One thing he had perfected as a young child was pick-pocketing. A bit like the Artful Dodger in Dickens's Oliver Twist. The staff door had a swipe card entry system. He followed the guard and pretended to be looking down at his programme, bumped into the guard, apologised and walked away.

He had the guard's swipe card. *That was too easy* he thought to himself. He then waited for the start of the next race and most people turned their attention to the race course. The noise of the crowd increased considerably and under this cover he moved towards the staff door.

The door opened easily and he slipped inside. The next few minutes were easy and he emerged a few minutes later dressed as a security guard, the uniform a little baggy on him but it would do.

The plan went like clockwork and half an hour later he was back behind the staff door with a money box. He forced it open and there was plenty of cash in there for what he wanted. Probably about £5,000 but he would count it later. He changed back into his own clothes, secreted the money in various pockets and calmly walk back out through the door. Having achieved what he came for, it was time to leave.

On the journey back home he spent some time planning what he was going to do with this new found liquidity. Nice hotel, fine dining, maybe some new clothes. After all, if you are going somewhere posh you gotta look posh, right?

# CHAPTER 18

DI Ralph Chamberlain wished he was here under completely different circumstances. He loved being outside in the first place but farmland and woods were his favourite. So many shades of green, interspersed with browns. The subtle, and sometimes not so subtle, signs that man was in control of the environment...or thought he was at least.

The sounds, as well as sights, made for a joyful experience in his opinion, be that the birds, farm animals, even the distant murmur of farm machinery had a certain music to it.

Then, the smells. They varied throughout the year, depending on growing seasons etc. There was something about the smell of freshly cut grass mixed with the unmistakeable aroma of cow shit. And when Chamberlain was around, the smell of burning pipe tobacco of course.

In a fair and perfect world he could see himself living in the countryside, wandering the fields and woods just with his own thoughts. Of course, if the world was perfect, it wouldn't be...*where had he heard that phrase*?

As he approached the top of the field his

thoughts came back to the reality of investigating two deaths and the likelihood that someone else had been involved…and wanted him to know it. Was it a personal vendetta? A crazed serial killer, who was likely to be a sociopath or psychopath. He would have to do some research to refresh his memory on the behaviour patterns of people with Antisocial Personality Disorder or APD as they now called it.

There was someone he knew he could talk to as well. Unfortunately that person was his DCI, Rebecca Flemming. He knew she had studied Psychology and Criminology in a previous life. He would have to grin and bear it for the greater good.

The tree line by the edge of the field was overgrown with low level scrub but there appeared to be a gap, part way along. He went through the gap carefully and found himself in a bit of a clearing, not visible if you were in the field but a reasonably large area clear of scrub. There appeared to be an indentation in the ground just back from the gap.

"Hmmm. What have we here?" he asked out loud, to no one but himself, giving another puff on his pipe.

He carefully walked around the clearing. He should really leave it to SOCOs to go over with a fine tooth Combe but he just wanted to get a feel for the place. His mind was now working overtime. His pipe had gone out. It looked like someone had been lying in the hollow. They would have a good view across the field and to the woods the other side.

*Why would someone go to the bother of covering their tracks with a herd of cows but not do anything about the clearing if they were coming back that way? Maybe they didn't actually come back this way. Maybe they just set the cows off across the field in the hope their tracks would be covered.*

This was looking more and more like a planned event, not just a loss of control moment.

# CHAPTER 19

Judith Webster was a little down today. Her last assignment had been very tedious. Important as it might be, reporting on village fetes or the Fire Service being called out for little Johnny who had got his head stuck in the school railing, again, was not exactly award winning journalism. This kind of parochial reporting didn't fire Judith up in the way that a big crime story or murder would.

Judith was in her early 30s, single and feeling a little despondent. She was sat in a cafe with her macchiato coffee, dreaming of Fleet Street. It could happen, right? She had had one juicy story in her career so far, the rest had been what she referred to as 'JJ' stories. Junior Journalist.

Her one claim to fame was following, and reporting on, the investigation into a major drug gang murder in Birmingham and she had had several articles printed in prime positions in the papers. But that was five years ago now. She needed something to get her teeth into, and PDQ! She had always hoped that her friend Rebecca Flemming would be able to put decent stories her way. She was quite senior in the local CID wasn't she? Nothing so far.

Her phone trilled, indicating a text received. That was spooky....it was from Rebecca! Just said 'Give me a call x'.

Judith perked up a little though it was probably just to arrange a girls night out which they hadn't done in a while. Never mind, she could remind Rebecca of her enormous journalistic talents and push for some dirt.

She finished her coffee, grabbed her stuff and exited the cafe. She rang Rebecca's mobile number.

"That was quick Jude! You must be really busy" she said sarcastically.

"Yeah, yeah, shut yer face, copper!" retorted Judith. "Are you angling for a drunken night out with your bestie then?"

"Sounds like a great idea but that will have to wait. I think I need your help. Would you come into the station for a chat as soon as you can?" Asked the DCI.

"Well, sure" said Judith. "I can come this afternoon, obviously having re-arranged my busy diary, and I'll bring some take out coffee 'cos last time you nearly poisoned me with the shit you have in the station!" She castigated.

"Yeah, fair comment. Ok I'll expect you in a while. Just get the desk sergeant to ring up for me". They ended their call and Judith wondered how on earth she could help her friend. Things were looking a little more positive.

With a lighter step she headed for her car in a nearby parking space. She had gone over the allowed time. She had a parking ticket. *Bollocks* she thought to herself. Maybe Rebecca would be able to cancel the ticket for her. She wanted *her* help after all.

The two women had known each other since university. Judith studied Journalism and Economics whilst her friend did Psychology and Criminology. They both knew which direction they want to take in terms of career, though in Judith's mind, her friend had done a lot better that she had so far.

There wasn't really any sense of competition between them but Judith couldn't help the niggle at the back of her thoughts that she was getting on a bit and needed to progress her career soon or she would be too old and on the shelf.

She was single, and currently happily so. Her last relationship had lasted all of 3 weeks after she discovered the man in question was seeing 2 other women at the same time as her. Not her kind of guy, as it turned out.

Pushing thoughts of the past aside, she got in her car and drove off, dreaming of front page stories and the accolades that would accompany them. Her little Fiat 500 was ideal for City driving. You could nip in and out of traffic and park in the smallest of spaces. Hers was a Sky Blue colour. She had chosen it against a red one. She always remembered her father telling her never to buy a red car. *Red is for danger* he would tell her. Probably nonsense but she had followed the advice anyway.

She lived in a pretty nice part of town. Warwick itself is not very big but adjoins Leamington Spa and is only just south of Birmingham. Her flat was in Shakespeare Avenue. Quite a main road but it gave easy access to all directions. Great Fish & Chip shop just down the road as well.

# CHAPTER 20

Having returned from Cheltenham to his flat, the killer went on the net and found a suitable hotel, booked a room for a couple of nights and then looked up menswear shops for a visit on the way to the hotel. There was a suitable one on the main road into the town where the hotel was situated. Ideal. On the bus route as well.

He gathered a few basics in an overnight bag and set off on his journey. He had left some of his ill-gotten gains behind, in a safe hiding place. He didn't want, nor need, to blow the whole lot at once.

Sitting on the bus his thoughts turned again to DI Chamberlain. He wondered if the connections had started clicking. He knew Chamberlain was no fool, but it was some time ago that they had *almost* met. He still seethed when he thought about the interruption to his project. He had spent a considerable amount of time on the planning of it, only to be foiled by Chamberlain inserting his size tens into the situation.

He had been close to being caught but had learned valuable lessons from the experience nonetheless. Still, he had been furious at the interruption. He had killed the first cat he saw on the way home after his escape. It didn't satisfy his urge to kill: he had killed many cats before but no humans. This was to be his first. Until that bastard Chamberlain came along.

It appeared to have helped Chamberlain's career no end. Promotion from PC to DC in CID and a transfer to the other side of the country. There he continued his rise and after 3 years was a Detective Sergeant. After a further 4 years he was promoted to Detective Inspector and returned to the CID section in his home town.

The psychopath had followed this progression closely. He had honed his own skills in the meantime and had killed several times. He had hidden these well as he hadn't wanted to be caught. That would have spoiled the real game of bringing down this bloody Chamberlain character.

He noticed his stop approaching, close to the clothes shop. He got off the bus and went in to the posh premises.

After about an hour, he came out again into the street. He looked very different. He was wearing a £500 suit, silk shirt, important looking tie and shiny new brogues. He had also bought a black fedora for good measure which now sat neatly on his head.

He had a thought. Maybe arriving by bus at the hotel didn't really fit in with the image he was trying to portray. *Taxi? ...Limousine!* Yes, much better. He searched on line on his smart phone and found a service not too far away. He could wait in a cafe if it was going to be too long arriving.

It all came together quite quickly and he found himself arriving at the posh hotel, the door of the limo being opened for him and his overnight bag being carried to the hotel entrance. He even tipped the driver. It made him feel good.

He put on an air of poshness…or at least what he thought was poshness. It seemed to work. The door was opened for him and his luggage, such as it was, carried for him. At the desk, a very polite young woman booked him in and gave him a key card for his room.

"I hope you enjoy your stay Sir. Anything you need just call down to us here at reception." She said sweetly.

"Thank you. And I shall!" He replied. He casually wondered to himself what it would be like to put his hands around her throat and squeeze until the life went out of her. He had never targeted women before. Maybe after the current project he would give that some thought.

He made his way to his room. *Very nice* he thought to himself. He undressed and hung the new clothes up neatly. He then went into the ensuite and stared at himself in the large mirror. *Still looking good* he praised himself.

He would have a shower and then relax for a while before getting dressed again for the evening meal. Maybe a drink in the bar first. Yes, good plan.

He would also write a note for DI Chamberlain

as he didn't seem to be catching on to the plot.

# CHAPTER 21

That same day, DI Chamberlain was seated in his DCI's office briefing her about the progress they were making and the tasks he had set for his team.

"Thank you Ralph" she said "Now as you know, I made a fool of myself at the press conference a few days ago and I need to recover that situation somehow. I have a very good friend who happens to be a local journalist."

"Do you now" grumped Chamberlain.

"Don't start. I know how you feel about the press but she is my friend and is a very good, honourable journalist. I trust her and I think she may be able to help me…us" she explained.

"I didn't know there was such a thing but whatever you say, M'am" Chamberlain said, unconvinced.

"She is due in to the station to see us any minute so I would like to introduce you and please be nice" pleaded his boss.

Chamberlain grunted. Just then her phone

rang. It was the desk sergeant announcing her friend's arrival.

A minute or two later there came a knock at the door.

"Come in" said Flemming.

The door opened and DS Harris poked his head in and said "I've got a Miss Webster here for you M'am".

"Yes, yes let her in Harris" said his DCI.

Judith Webster entered her office with such a smile on her face that DI Chamberlain immediately lost all thoughts of animosity towards such a member of the press. His DCI noticed the look on his face.

"Judith, great to see you and thanks for coming in at such short notice. Can I introduce you to my Detective Inspector Ralph Chamberlain? I must warn you though, he is very grumpy when it comes to dealing with journalists" she said mischievously.

Chamberlain stood and held out his hand. "Nice to meet you Miss Webster….and don't listen to her, she's just winding you, and me, up" he said. They shook hands and he felt her warm skin as they grasped, perhaps just a little longer than strictly necessary. The touch felt nice to Chamberlain,

She smiled and withdrew her hand, demurely. "My pleasure" she said simply and took the seat offered by her friend.

"So what can I do to help you Rebecca?" asked

Judith.

"Ok, so everything we tell you about this case we are on is strictly confidential unless we say otherwise. I may have to give you details that we do not want known to the public. However, since my disastrous press conference the other day, there is some damage limitation required. It turns out that we probably have a third person involved in the *Poachers Feud* as it was labelled by the press. Possibly even a serial killer." Explained the DCI.

"Can I just interrupt you there, Ma'm. On the evidence we had at the time, it was not an unreasonable assumption that these two had killed each other, strange as it may sound. Anything else is still conjecture. The new evidence we have may be coincidence or someone playing silly buggers....pardon my French" he said, looking across at the Journalist. "We have a long way to go before we can confirm that, we have no suspects for example" he added.

"Yes, I understand all that Ralph but it still remains that we have to tell people that the case is now re-opened and enquiries will resume, at pace I may add" responded the DCI.

"Ok, so if I read this correctly Rebecca, you want me to help you release this new information in a way that doesn't make you look like a load of plonkers?" Suggested Judith.

Both of the other people in the room winced slightly but she had hit the nail on the head really.

"Yes" said Flemming, simply.

"Ok, can I suggest that you decide on what details you want to release and I will go away and give it some thought as to how I will present the situation to your adoring public." Said Judith.

Chamberlain was quietly impressed as to this woman's obvious appreciation of the situation and her wisdom as to how to proceed. He hadn't expected that.

"Splendid" said Flemming. "Can we meet up again tomorrow then and decide on how to proceed?".

Once final pleasantries had been exchanged, Judith left the office and headed back out of the station, already thinking of angles that could save the face of the force.

Back in the office, Flemming looked at Chamberlain and raised an eyebrow in a knowing way.

"With the utmost respect, piss off Ma'm" said Chamberlain.

"I didn't say a word, though I did notice the way you were looking at her" pleaded Flemming defensively, holding up both hands in front of her.

"Yeah, yeah, I know that only young, fit, well

off, attractive men are allowed to eye up attractive young women" said Chamberlain, sarcastically.

"Well you can't expect to be all of those, Ralph" said Flemming with a grin.

"Oh, and which of those am I not in your female opinion?" Chamberlain was a little ruffled now.

"Oh I couldn't tell you that, you'd be big headed and insecure at the same time" she replied.

"Hmmph" was all Chamberlain could manage.

"Worth keeping her on our side though, don't you think?....and I'll let that insubordination go, just this once". She was smiling.

# CHAPTER 22

After a brief meeting in the squad room, Chamberlain and Harris went off to have another look at the crime scene. Chamberlain had tasked Dixon and Norrish with going back over what they had so far and then looking further into the backgrounds of the few people they had come into contact with so far, namely the Barman and the Farmer. It was all they had to go on at the moment. He also asked them to catch up with forensics and pathology and give his apologies to both of them.

They took Chamberlains car but he let Harris drive so that he could get his pipe out and smoke it safely on the way. He was still slight sore from the other night.

As they drove along, he tried to keep his mind o the case but his thoughts kept returning to that journalist. *Ridiculous* he thought. Though she was very attractive in his opinion. *Stop it* he scolded himself.

"Sir?" Harris had been trying to get his boss's attention.

"What? Yes?" Said Chamberlain, returning to

the real world.

"I was just thinking. It could still be that they killed each other couldn't it?" Said Harris.

"Yes" puff, "Yes indeed" puff, puff went Chamberlain. "Someone quite innocent could have been lying in that depression, watching the cows, and along come two poachers who have a fight and kill each other. This other person then goes to the scene of the deaths, steals one glove off the dead body of one of the poachers and then takes it to near where I live and throws it into my garden, just for shits and giggles....?" conjectures Chamberlain.

"Yeah, well, if you put it like that it does seem a little unlikely" said Harris, meekly.

"In all seriousness, we can't rule anything out at this point Tommy boy. Let's go and have another look, bearing in mind our new hypotheses" said Chamberlain, to placate his Sergeant.

They left the car in the lay-by and headed up the overgrown path. It was a little easier now as quite a few people involved in the investigation had been up and down the path in the course of their duties. Nothing they could do about that now.

They reached the scene of the deaths a few minutes later. It was a dry day with a light breeze. They were grateful for the conditions. Searching round an outdoor crime scene in anything other than dry conditions was a nightmare, and made it difficult to assess what was around.

There were now only remnants of police tape. There would be more once the SOCOs got back on site again but for now it looked like a very sad place. Chamberlain guessed that it was a very sad place for the relatives of the two that had died.

Chamberlain noticed the cows were not in the field this time. Being milked maybe? Or just rotated to another field perhaps. No matter. He had explained to the team about his conversation with the farmer. His two DCs would no doubt go over that again when they interviewed the man. It would be interesting to see if they got the same answers that he had. Same with the Barman. The two young DCs might not get different information but maybe additional facts and ideas on a second go.

"Ok, let's not disturb this area any more than necessary. The SOCOs won't thank us for sure. I want to see if the path goes much further into the woods and where it ends up" said Chamberlain.

"Right behind you Sir." Answered Harris.

They followed the overgrown path though the woods, snagging on bramble branches that were infringing on the route. Both sustained a few scratches to their hands and Harris got one across the nose when it sprung back in Chamberlains wake. He said nothing, just soldiered on.

After a while they reached a sort of clearing in the woods. They had passed the end of the field where the cows had been and were now a little disorientated if they were honest.

"Bread crumbs" said Chamberlain, quietly to himself.

"What was that sir?" Asked Harris.

"Nothing Tom, let's just not get lost out here. It would be very embarrassing." Said Chamberlain.

"Oh that's not a problem sir. I have a GPS app on my phone" answered Harris confidently.

"Of course you do" said the technophobe, begrudgingly.

They carried on across the clearing and found where the path continued. Eventually they came to a stile that led to another field. Cows. Were they the same ones thought Chamberlain? He decided they would look on the map later to see how the surrounding area fitted in and what other access routes there were.

"Ok let's go back. I have a feel for the area now" said Chamberlain.

They headed back down the path. They got to the clearing and Chamberlain suddenly stopped. They were viewing the clearing from a different aspect and he had noticed something. Might be nothing. However, it appeared that there were some similar looking mounds in the earth dotted around the clearing. Ancient settlement ruins perhaps. Remnants of bomb craters from the Second World War? They were fairly close to Birmingham which had received its' fair share of bombing during the Blitz.

"Tom, do you notice anything about this clearing that wasn't apparent on our way up?" Asked Chamberlain.

Harris looked around for a few moments. "Mounds" he said simply.

"Quite" said his boss. "We'd better get the SOCOs and a cadaver dog up here just in case. They could be ancient burial mounds or they could be more recent."

He reckoned there were about half a dozen of these mounds, randomly dotted about. He felt a chill go through his body.

"Let's get back" he said.

# CHAPTER 23

The psycho killer was on his second day of his mini break. Loving the hotel and the meal he had the previous night had been spectacular. If that was how posh people lived he wanted more of it.

He felt he had acted the part well, with enough aloofness and expectation of good service for a posh person. It had seemed to work. The staff had been quite obsequious in their service to him. He supposed they were paid fairly well for it. It was a new experience for him. His childhood had been anything but posh. Painful.

He reflected on his parents attitude towards him. Indifference? As strong as hate? Maybe his mother. His father was just a waste of space. At the times he couldn't avoid it, his wife would hit him, with or without the aid of utensils. Their son watched, fascinated.

He didn't escape the violence. When his father was unavailable , his mother's anger would turn on him. He never really knew what, if anything, he had done wrong. It was just the way things were. His mother was angry. She hit him. He hit small animals. The cycle of violence.

He had taken another shower. Why not take full advantage of the facilities? He now lay on the bed, wrapped in a bath robe...one of the hotel's of course. He started to think over his crusade against DI Chamberlain....*bastard*.

Time he stepped up and turned up the heat. He wanted to kill again but how could he make it obvious that this was all directed at Chamberlain. There was, of course, the option to kill the man himself. There would be a certain amount of satisfaction in this. He probably would eventually, but not just yet. He wanted the man to suffer for a while, like he had suffered all these years.

A thought came to him. The women that was in the garden when he threw the glove over the fence. She must be connected to Chamberlain in some way. He wasn't married or have a girlfriend, and to be honest she looked a bit old for the inspector.

A bit of research and maybe a stake out. That was a plan. He would set things in motion when he got back from his little holiday. He filed that thought away and started to think about what he was going to do for the rest of the day. A swim. Another shower. Dinner, drinks, then bed. Sorted.

The swim made him feel virtuous. The hotel pool was big enough for the several lengths he swam to get the blood pumping round his body and give him a sense of having worked out and done his body some good.

The shower freshened him up, ready to dress again in the posh clothes he was rather getting used to wearing. He might buy some others it there was enough cash left from his race day exploits. Or if necessary he could do it again. Different race course.

The diner and drinks made him feel a little bloated and slightly light headed. He had a gin and tonic before the meal and most of a bottle of Macon Rouge with his delicious, perfectly cooked Cote du Boeuf.

He was definitely ready for his bed when he got back to his room. He hung up the suit in the wardrobe, so as not to crease it, and left the rest of his clothes neatly on the armchair in the corner. The new brogues had rubbed slightly but they would wear in after a while, he was certain.

As soon as he got into bed and his head hit the pillow, he fell asleep and dreamt of cows.

# CHAPTER 24

The next morning, Chamberlain and Flemming were due to meet up again with Judith Webster to decide on damage limitation. Chamberlain had just arrived at the station when he bumped into his DCI rushing out of the doors on her way to the carpark.

"Ah Ralph, really sorry but I have been summoned up to HQ for a high level meeting. I can't get out of it. Can you handle Judith on your own?" She said.

"Do I have a choice?" Asked Chamberlain.

The DCI didn't respond, just giving him an eyebrows up look as she rushed past him.

"Thought not" Chamberlain said out loud, to himself. He had about half an hour before the allotted meeting time so he though he would pop in to the incident room and catch up with the team. He knew if anything important had turned up Harris would have rung him but it did no harm to show his face.

"Morning!" He announced himself as he went through the door.

He was greeted by some surprised faces. They didn't usually expect their boss to come in to the office if he could help it. He explained his presence and asked if there were any updates or developments.

"Not really Sir." Said DS Harris. "We have some more witness statements and interviews to do today so hopefully that will bring something out of the woodwork"

"Ok. I have a meeting with a journalist….Yes I know, my favourite people…DCI Flemming wants to try to limit the damage done by us closing the case too early and she thinks this women can help. A friend of hers it appears." Explained Chamberlain.

He wondered if he had time to pop out for a few puffs of his pipe. He had a fresh tin of tobacco and that always tasted a little nicer than when it had been opened for a while. A phone rang in the room. Harris picked it up and muttered a few words into the mouthpiece.

"Your date is here Sir" he said to Chamberlain, with a wry smile on his face.

Chamberlain frowned. "Watch it Harris" he said…then grinned back at him.

He made sure his shirt was tucked in, his trousers pulled up and his tie straight and with a flourish for the benefit of the room, he departed and went to meet Miss Webster.

She was a little early but he liked that in a person. He could not abide people being late, though he was occasionally guilty of the crime himself sometimes.

They went Ito an empty room just down the corridor from the incident room. It was unused so only contained a couple of tables and 3 chairs.

"Welcome to our luxury meeting lounge" quipped Chamberlain. He hope the meeting wouldn't take long so they shouldn't be too uncomfortable.

"Well, thank you Inspector" said Webster with a smile, sitting herself in one of the chairs. She couldn't quite fathom this policeman yet but give it time. He intrigued her. If only she had known, the same thoughts were going through Chamberlain's mind about her.

"I'm afraid DCI Flemming has been called away so won't be joining us. She has left it to us to come up with a plan of attack" he said.

*Interesting choice of words* the journalist thought to herself. *He obviously sees the media as the enemy.*

"No problem. I have given it some thought and I think honesty is the best way forward rather than trying to put a spin on it" said Webster, looking him in the eye.

*Refreshing* he thought to himself. He was wary of journalists and the media as a whole. Yes they had their uses but they were uncontrollable in his experience and could easily ruin an investigation by jumping the gun or printing stories that were way off the mark.

"Good" he said. "I agree. We were acting in good faith based on the evidence we had at the time. I must say though, it wasn't helped by the story that appeared so quickly in one of the local papers about the Poacher's Feud Tragedy"

"No, well, that wasn't me" she said defensively. She crossed her legs and looked at him defiantly.

The Police Forces in the UK have dedicated Media and Press Offices from which they control the information they want fed to the public. The timing of these releases is sometimes critical but can also produce very helpful results. They are not keen on the Media taking things into their own hands, especially if information comes direct from the public and bypasses them.

If only they had known, that in this case, the early printing of the sensational headline about the deaths, had prompted our psychopath's intervention with the glove and was the first crumb on the trail of clues in the search for him.

"Ok, well if you could draft something and send it through to Rebecca, that would be great" said Chamberlain.

"I will" she said back. "You don't like me very

much do you inspector" she continued, looking a little sad he thought.

"I don't know you" he said simply.

"Ha, well you could have said 'don't be silly, of course I do' but then that isn't your style is it" she challenged.

"I don't know how to respond to that" He said. He was feeling a little uncomfortable now.

"Oh come on detective it's a brave new world. All the old stereotypes and cliches are out of the window now" said Judith.

"There is a reason for stereotypes and cliches you know" Chamberlain rebuffs, sadly.

"Ok, point taken. Let's have dinner and talk about this some more" she said boldly. Chamberlain was taken aback. "No strings, I think the saying goes" she smiled and Chamberlain was immediately in love, though he wasn't fully conscious of the fact.

He had been single for so long that he had forgotten how to behave in a flirty situation. This was definitely one of those situations….he thought it was at any rate.

"Ha ha Ok, as long as you treat me gently" he said jokingly. Was that a glint in her eyes he saw? *She is forward* he thought to himself.

# CHAPTER 25

He had some time before his boss would return and he could update her. He went outside to the carpark after Judith Webster had left and resorted to his trusty pipe and baccy again. They had agreed to go for a meal at the end of the week and had exchanged numbers in order to make fuller arrangements later. *What am I doing?* He thought.

His last relationship had ended amicably and was something like 8 years ago now. The two of them just hadn't had time for each other and had drifted apart. It was sad but inevitable. She travelled a lot for her work and he was always being called out on cases and couldn't commit to specific times for them to spend time together. He gathered she had now moved to the USA now, He didn't really think about her very often these days, until now.

Was he reading this women, Judith, correctly? Or was he about to make a monumental prat out of himself. Probably the latter.

He saw his boss's car pull into the station carpark. She pulled into her reserved space and got out of the car. Seeing him she walked over to where he was leant against the wall of the building.

"Well, well, well, you sly old dog you" she mocked. "You move fast don't you? I had no idea you had it in you".

Clearly news travelled fast. Judith Webster must have rung her friend as soon as she left the meeting and told her about the dinner date.

"Referring to the previously aforementioned respect, boss....piss off!" Said Chamberlain. He shouldn't have been surprised really. He knew women were always keen to share information about flirtations and dates. He, on the other hand, would rather die that let his team know what he was up to.

His boss merely laughed and proceeded Ito the building and up towards her office. Chamberlain followed like an obedient puppy.

Once they were seated in her office she informed Chamberlain that Judith had also told her of the plan re the damage limitation and she had approved.

"I have someone else I think you should talk to... another friend. Don't worry, this one is a man" she said grinning at her senior detective.

"Right" he said cautiously. "Who and why and where?"

"Professor Richard Phillips, a senior lecturer at the university in Criminology and Psychology. We studied together and he stayed on in academia." She explained.

"You think we might have a serial killer or psychopath, don't you?" He asked, not really wanting to hear the answer.

"We have to keep an open mind of course, but even if we don't have a serial killer and it's a one off, the psychology of a killer can be a complicated subject to untangle" said Flemming.

"Ok, I am happy to meet your friend and have a chat" agreed Chamberlain.

"I hoped you would so I have told him you will be at his office at the university tomorrow morning and 9.30am" directed Flemming.

"Yes Ma'm" acceded Chamberlain.

Detecting a little reluctance from her DI, the senior officer gave him a quizzical look.

"Ralph, my learning on the subject was nearly 20 years ago so I am a bit rusty but we all know that not all killers are psychopaths and not all psychopaths are killers. Serial killers, on the other hand, are usually suffering from some kind of antisocial personality disorder. It will do no harm for you to get updated on the latest research and thinking from an expert in his field" she expanded.

"Yes, fair enough" he replied. "I just wonder if we are jumping the gun a little. It may still be that the newspaper headline was right and it was tragic feud between two competing poachers. The business with the glove may be some joker trying to get in on the investigation for their own warped reasons. We haven't actually had it confirmed by forensics that it is a matching glove."

"Well, chase them up will you? You can always cancel the meeting if it turns out not to be a match." Said the DCI.

They parted in agreement and Chamberlain went to seek out Harris. He found him in the canteen, drinking a poor excuse for a coffee. He was looking down at his phone, absorbed in something, so he didn't see his boss approaching.

"Bloody teenagers, always looking at their phones and not where they are going." Jibed Chamberlain.

"Ah, Sir, sorry, I was just checking my emails" pleaded Harris.

DI Chamberlain did have a smart phone but he hadn't quite got as far as setting it up for emails. Calls and texts were about his limit. He relied on his team to update him with important developments re any current case and he didn't really use email for personal communications.

"Just kidding you Tom." He said to his junior. "Any news from Forensics or Pathology for me?"

"Yes, actually. They have matched the two gloves and have determined that there is animal blood and human blood on both of them. They are waiting to match the blood to one or both of the victims." Said Harris, obviously pausing.

"Hmm" grumbled Chamberlain. It looked like he would be off to the university tomorrow after all. "You have more?"

"Yea Sir. Professor Reed is of the opinion that Ronald Denton would have been unable to deliver such a decisive stab to Charles Foxborough whilst choking and grabbing at his throat to try and free himself. And also that if the sequence was reversed, Foxborough would have been unable to make the noose so immovable and secure if he had such a stab wound." Harris relayed. "However, neither can, so far, provide any evidence for a third party being involved so if there was someone else, they were very careful and aware of forensic procedures." He concluded.

Chamberlain thought for a few moments. It looked like this case was going to be more complicated than they first thought. His right hand was curled around his pipe in his pocket, sub-consciously.

"Ok Tom, we need to find a suspect, urgently. Get the team to go back over the two victims' histories. Talk to family, friends. Work associates etc. I'll go to the pub again and talk to the barman,,,,what is his name?" Chamberlain asked.

"Err...Brian Jones" said Harris.

"Right. After that I'll go and find that farmer again and get more details about the surrounding fields and woods. Have the cadaver dogs been up there yet?" Enquired the DI.

" Due up there this afternoon sir, so you might bump into them if you go up to see the farmer." Said Harris.

"Righto" Chamberlain left his DS in the canteen and headed out of the building. He headed towards the pub, on foot. It would give him time for a leisurely smoke and to go over things in his head.

# CHAPTER 26

In his flat, the killer was staring at an article in the newspaper. The same paper that had printed the annoying headline that had upset him so. He sat now reading the retraction and apology that a certain Judith Webster had written, following a face to face meeting with the senior officers involved with the case. *A bit pally with the police aren't we?* He thought to himself.

The short article simply read:

'Local Police have re-opened their investigation into the death of two men earlier this week. Following a meeting with senior officers, I can vouch for their determination to discover what happened to these men. Their previous statement, by DCI Flemming, was based on the evidence they had at the time. New evidence has apparently come to their attention which has led to the re-opening of the case. Judith Webster, Current Affairs reporter.' A small picture of her was inserted next to the article.

*Well that's very scant information* he thought. No mention of his clever flourish with the glove. How annoying. They appeared to be playing their cards close to their chests.

Perhaps he should investigate this reporter. She might be able to help him, unknowingly, with his project. Things didn't seem to be going his way and certainly not fast enough to satisfy his yearning desire to engage in the game with DI Ralph Chamberlain.

He had her name and her place of work and knew what she looked like from the picture next to the article. It would be easy to follow her and find out where she lived. A stake out. That would be fun. He was good at those. He got ready for the mission. No need for a disguise at this point. Nobody knew who he was. He would just innocently hang around the newspaper's offices and then follow her. He would have to be a little more careful than usual. He knew women tended to be more aware of their surroundings and had an innate fear of being followed or stalked *for good reason* he thought to himself.

His first foray was unsuccessful. There was no sign of her. He tried again the next day. Success. She left work a little earlier than he would have thought and he followed her home, keeping his car a few behind hers so as not to draw attention. It was tricky in the traffic but he managed it. She went into her block of flats and he sat outside watching for a while. She might now be in for the night but he waited a little longer. His patience was rewarded.

About an hour and a half later she came out again and appeared to be dressed up to the nines. He followed again and she went towards the centre of town, parked on the street and headed for a restaurant. Meal out eh?

He was just reminiscing about his posh nosh at the hotel he had stayed at when he saw someone he was not expecting at all. DI Ralph Chamberlain. He watched them greet each other and sit themselves at a table in the restaurant. Oh yes, very pally with the police indeed! He wondered if this was a date or just a meeting. A date, he hoped. For then he could use the relationship in his scheme to get to DI Chamberlain. Oh yes, this was developing in a very interesting direction.

# CHAPTER 27

What our artful psychopath didn't know was that the racecourse, the source of his current funding, was progressing well in their investigations. It hadn't taken long to discover that money was missing. The empty box in the Staff Only area and the very irate Bookie who thought he had had a great day discovering that he was considerably short on the day's profit.

Once these facts had come to light they had called in the local police. Their CCTV footage had been carefully reviewed and they had identified a mystery person who could be seen entering the STAff ONLY area in civilian clothes, exiting the same door in a security guard uniform and then shortly afterwards going back through the same door carrying a money box. He then comes out again back in civilian clothing and the box is later found empty.

They can't identify the man as he looks down most of the time and the cameras are at some elevation. He is also wearing a security guards baseball cap. They are now studying any CCTV footage they can get from outside of the racecourse to see if they can follow the mystery man and ascertain in which direction he is heading, either in his own vehicle or on public transport.

This is as far as they have got so far but they are persevering in the hood of catching the thief if not recovering the money. They have told the bookie that this is unlikely even if they find the man.

A description, as far as it goes, has been circulated on the Police National Computer system, together with the CCTV footage. They know it's a long shot but they have to try. They will also do a TV appeal using the same material. You never know!

The killer is, so far, unaware of how reckless he has been. His assumption had been that if he managed the theft and escaped the racecourse, then it would be almost impossible to trace him.

What he hadn't allowed for was all the other members of the public using their mobile phones as video cameras. The police hoped that someone would come forward once they saw the appeal. Again a long shot but this was becoming a common tool when trying to identify perpetrators of all sorts of crime from shoplifting to driving offences. It just sometimes took longer for this information to surface.

The investigators did know that even if they were able to get an image of the thief face, they wouldn't necessarily be able to identify him. It would probably mean another appeal and the usual circulation among the forces in the UK. Much police work took patience and time and many man hours, and woman hours of course.

The appeal appeared on the local news and

they started to get dozens of phone calls with offers of video footage from the day of the theft. This was going to take a huge amount of resources to sift through. They just hoped they would get lucky. They did.

A young couple was enjoying their fist trip to a race course and she was filming as much of it as she could. She happened to be filming her boyfriend just as the fake security guard was coming out of the STAFF ONLY door. He was only in the frame for about 2 seconds and the couple hadn't noticed him at all. However, they had seen the appeal and had sent in all the clips they had for the day. The poor PC who was given the job of going through all the clips had been on the verge of fallen asleep on the job when he caught a glimpse of the man they were looking for.

It was not a great view of the man's face but their tech services had done their best to enhance it and had produced some stills as well as the original clip. These had now been circulated throughout the force and they now had to wait.

# CHAPTER 28

On the morning of his dinner date with Judith Webster, Chamberlain had been to the university for his meeting with Professor Richard Phillips. It had been a useful meeting, very illuminating. The Professor obviously knew his subjects.

On arriving at the academic's office, Chamberlain had been welcomed by a friendly yet learned face.

"DI Chamberlain, welcome. I gather from Rebecca that you need a short course on loony murderers." said Phillips.

Chamberlain was rather taken aback by the terminology. He hadn't expected such an expert in his field to be so flippant about the subject. He didn't mind particularly but it put him off his stride somewhat.

"Err yes, hi, nice to meet you" he replied, obviously non-plussed.

"Relax Inspector, and I apologise for my irreverent tone. It helps me sometimes when dealing with these things" explained the Professor. "How can I help? Rebecca tells me you may have a psychopathic killer on your hands."

"Well, possibly jumping the gun a little. We don't know for sure yet but there are some oddities about the case. I guess she felt it was worth getting ahead of the game" said Chamberlain.

"Fair enough, fair enough" said the Professor. "I am happy to give you a few words of guidance just in case it turns out Rebecca is correct. Tell me what you know so far".

Chamberlain outlined the case for the professor including the details they had so far about the victims, the location, the causes of death, the lack of forensics and finally the curious delivery of the matching glove.

"My word. Very Sherlock Holmesian." Said Phillips.

Chamberlain winced at the mention of the fictitious sleuth who always seemed to make Scotland Yard look like idiots.

"As you say" continued Phillips "Not conclusive but enough to raise the question I would say. Let me tell you a few things about people with Antisocial Personality Disorders. There are different types, as you may be aware. Not all killers are psychopaths and not all psychopaths are killers. Not all psychopaths are violent. Some are even considered good human beings. Studies have found there are 'successful psychopaths' who are more likely to be promoted

THE WOODLAND PATH MURDERS

to leadership positions and less likely to serve time behind bars.....” He stopped abruptly. “We could be a while here. I’ll get some coffee organised. He spoke into a phone briefly and then sat back and continued. *Academics love speaking about their subject* thought Chamberlain to himself.

The professor sat forward again and seemed to go into lecture mode.

“Although both biological and environmental factors play a role in the development of psychopathy and sociopathy, many agree that, psychopathy is chiefly a genetic or inherited condition, notably related to the underdevelopment of parts of the brain responsible for emotional regulation and impulse control are commonly marred with **childhood** abuse and **trauma**. This can sometimes mean that as a child, so much pain was experienced, and to an extent, normalised, that their own habits and view of who they are have been shaped by it. Humans are creatures of habit, and so the violence experienced as a child could easily resurface as an adult, often referred to as the cycle of violence. The periods of abuse could also function as mental milestones, and so re-experiencing violence could become a means of reassuring themselves of their own **identity**. As an adult, this person might continue to deliver and experience the violence upon themselves, or decide to deliver it upon others. A masochist who sublimates the experience of pain through another body becomes a sadist. The feelings of helplessness when they were abused as a child might also motivate them to switch roles and change the power differential. Having complete power over another individual is also indicative of a sadist."

There was a knock at the door. "Ah, coffee. Come in" shouted the Professor.

A tray of coffee and biscuits was delivered and place on the Professors desk. Neither men took much notice and the coffee sat there and began to get cold.

"You say there doesn't appear to be any sexual motive in these killings. It's not uncommon but it makes it more difficult to work out the true motive" said Phillips. He continued, "When interviewed, if caught or thought a suspect, they will usually try to divert the blame by claiming that, for example, they like women, or even respect them. Saying you respect women is a bit of a red flag. Respect should be individually earned and not because of your gender label so it probably means it is important to the psychopath that *he* is respected - it would be more normal to say that you wouldn't harm or rape a women, or a man come to that".

Chamberlain felt the Professor was wandering a bit in his advice so tried to bring him back on track.

"So how do I catch him if we do decide we have a psychopath on our hands?" asked Chamberlain.

"I don't really know, to be honest Inspector. I think, as with any crime I guess, you have to hope that they make a mistake somewhere along the line and give you some breadcrumbs to follow." said Phillips.

"All this sounds very stereotypical" said Chamberlain.

"This might be a little contentious but there is a reason there are stereotypes and cliches. They both have negative connotations and can be frowned upon in writing, speech and actions. But within the human race there are people who don't want to stand out and be individual, they find comfort in the crowd. One shouldn't therefore necessarily be offended by these collective nouns. Cliches are not necessarily a bad thing either. We tend to hang on to things we recognise, good and bad. There is a kind of comfort in that recognition. I'm not saying they are all good either by the way! I guess it is the way they are used that counts and I think you could say it is narrow-minded to label them always bad or negative to the fabric of society".

This was not entirely what Chamberlain was hoping for but it looked like the Professor had more to say so he just raised his eyebrows, appealing for more information. He wasn't wrong.

"If you do think you have someone with APD, for example if more victims turn up, then I certainly have some guidance as to how to deal with them. The most evident weakness a psychopath presents is their own abnormally large ego. They demonstrate impulsive and irresponsible lifestyles, take risks, are irresponsible and unreliable, financially parasitic, and have a lack of realistic, long-term goals." expanded Phillips.

"That's a lot to get my head around, Professor" said Chamberlain.

"Well, as you say, you don't know for sure if this is what you are dealing with but at least you may understand that such people are complicated and very dangerous. If you do find a suspect then I would advise extreme caution when talking to them. Keep your emotions in check, don't let them think you are intimidated in any way. They are great liars, so don't fall for their stories. They will try and talk about you but don't let them, turn the conversation back onto them." These words from Phillips were said with some passion so he clearly felt they were very important.

"I think that is probably enough for you for now Inspector but at least you have some grounding in the matter. I could go on for hours but I expect most of it wouldn't sink in" said Phillips.

*I''m sure you could, and I'm sure you are right* thought Chamberlain.

"But remember, the event of killing is extremely important to a psychopathic serial killer, which tells you that they have a lot invested in the experience." finished off the Professor.

That appeared to be the end of the lesson so Chamberlain thanked the Professor and left the office, and the university. Pipe time.

Sherlock Holmesian, the professor had said. DI Chamberlain was a little cynical about the plethora of famous fictional literary Detectives, such as Sherlock Holmes, Hercule Poirot and the more modern ones like Morse, Frost and Inspector George Gently. He was more interested in true historical detectives who had paved the way for how he did his job now. They had helped develop techniques and ways of thinking that revolutionised crime fighting. The way forensics had grown, DNA and other techniques. Not simply a lucky leap of deduction, though the odd lucky break didn't hurt.

He wondered how they had managed without all the modern tools of crime fighting. No wonder there were wrongful arrests and miscarriages of justice. It was pretty certain that quite a few people had been wrongly hanged for crimes they didn't commit and also a lot of murderers must have got away with their crimes.

He had studied many old cases and the methods that the SIOs, as they are called now, had managed their work. For example, he had a lot of

SIMON FORD

respect for Detective Chief Inspector Walter Dew and his partner Detective Mitchel who investigated the disappearance of singer Cora Crippen in 1910. Dew had been investigating crime for about 3 decades when he was assigned the Crippen case and had previously been involved in the hunt for Jack The Ripper. Whenever he had a big murder case he had terrible insomnia. His instinct told him something was wrong when he first met Dr. Crippen. In the end, his persistence in searching Crippen's house paid off and Cora's body was found buried in the basement of the property.

Dr. Crippen's behaviour and tell tale signs kept DI Dew on the scent of the crime. He knew something was wrong and kept going.

Dr. Crippen tried to disguise the identity of the body by cutting it up, removing certain parts and covering the remains with lime. When dry, lime dissolves flesh but he had mixed it wet and it then becomes a preserver. A major mistake on the murderers part. It meant easy identification of Cora's remains.

All crime fighting relies on criminals making mistakes and detectives develop a certain intuition after doing the job of an investigator for a period of time. Chamberlain hoped he was getting such an intuition. He certainly needed it with this current case.

He made his way back to Warwick Town via the A46 and then turned off onto then Coventry Road. As he got closer to the town, he passed Warwick

Hospital on his right and then he could see Priory park, which was now a reserve and educational centre. There was a lot of history associated with The Priory, going back hundreds of years. Some famous guy whose name Chamberlain couldn't remember.

The traffic built as he approached the Northgate and the police station that contained his office and the incident room. When he had parked up, he sat in his car for a while, window one, pipe smoke billowing, thinking about what the professor had told him. He wasn't sure whether it would be of any use to him but no harm, no foul.

He was looking forward to his dinner date with Judith Webster later that day. He had better check in to the office, deal with whatever needed dealing with and then get home and get ready for tonight. Should he wear a suit? Or dress smart/casual? The latter, he thought, would be more appropriate. Not overpowering but not sloppy. *Bloody hell, what's happening to me* he thought to himself.

# CHAPTER 29

As she read the menu, Chamberlain looked at her over the top of his. *Ridiculous notion.* His natural cynicism leapfrogged over the vain thought she might be interested in him. He thought of his brother David, married, two kids. He was a teacher at a Secondary School somewhere on the outskirts of Manchester. He saw him at Christmas, usually. Or funerals of elderly relatives. He had married young and got on with the process of life, making a career and a family at the same time. Chamberlain had managed the career bit but not the family side of it.

His parents, Lyn and Robert Chamberlain, tended not to nag him about it, for which he was grateful. *In your own good time, son,* his father would say. *Got to be the right girl* his mother would follow with.

Judith looked up suddenly and caught him looking at her.

"Any famous ancestors in the political arena then?" she asked.

"Ah… great grandfather Neville…ha ha no, no relation I'm afraid" he answered, glad to cover his embarrassment at being caught looking at her. "My grandfather was a teacher and my father worked for the government at GCHQ. Actually, I don't know what my Great-Grandfather did but it wasn't politics" he filled in the information for her.

She raised her eyebrows at the part about GCHQ. She was sure some juicy stories would come out of that place. "Probably a good thing, you'd forever be ribbed about the 'I have a piece of paper in my hand' thing he said, which turned out to be bollocks. Some people actually think he was holding his shopping list" she said mockingly.

"Well quite" replied Chamberlain. "I think he also promised 'Peace for our time' just before World War Two broke out. I'm glad I am not related, I was never a big fan of politicians."

"Nor Journalists, I gather from Rebecca" there was a teasing expression on Judith's face as she let fly this salvo.

"Hmmm, well…I, errr…Thanks for *that* DCI Flemming" he said forcefully.

They both laughed. He noted that her face lit up when she laughed. *Stop it* he told himself. She was slight of figure, long chestnut brown hair framing a pretty face with sparkling eyes. She didn't wear much makeup, just enough to highlight her cheeks and lips.

"I have had some unfortunate experiences with journalists over the years, so my view is coloured somewhat. Having said that, I am open to persuasion that I am wrong" said Chamberlain. *Smooth or creepy?*

"Well, I am good at putting my point of view but maybe tonight is not the time for confrontation" she came back with.

They agreed to steer away from politics and journalism and had a very pleasant meal, easy conversation, perhaps aided by the wine they had with the food.

Chamberlain told her about his likes and dislikes. Likes being music, in particular Genesis and the prog rock genre, fishing, when he had the time, watching rugby and his pipes. He also told her of his love of architecture and archaeology.

"I have just got back from Barcelona. Fascinating city" he said. He relayed a little about the history of the city, the Roman influence and finally the Modernisme of Gaudi.

She seemed interested and he found it easy to talk about himself for once. She laughed when he told her his dislikes, being semolina, couscous and gardening.

"Semolina and couscous are pointless unless you put something tasty with them" he explained. "Then you may as well just eat the tasty things!"

She was also quite free with her conversation about herself. She was 34, single, terrible at choosing boyfriends and had always wanted to be a journalist. She liked swimming, especially in the sea, reading, she could take or leave couscous and also was not fond of semolina, nor rice pudding. She didn't have her own garden but thought she might quite like to see things grow.

"My parents lived in Sussex. They nearly got divorced a few years ago but decided not to, in the end. There was no one else involved, as far as I know, but I think things got a bit stale after I left home. My Dad was a newspaper man and met my Mum when they both worked on the Surrey Times, many years ago. I think she was a copy writer, he was a photographer. We lost him over two years ago now" she explained.

"So it's in the blood then, this journalism thing" said Chamberlain.

"Thing?" she said, slightly affronted. "It's my living, if you don't mind" she was trying not to grin.

"Sorry, I didn't mean to belittle what you do" begged Chamberlain.

They had desserts and then coffee and time seemed to fly past. Chamberlain found himself smiling a lot. She was very easy to be with. She was lovely to be with. *Oh boy, what's happening.*

What they didn't know was that they were being watched by an ever increasingly angry psychopathic killer. How dare they be enjoying themselves and each others company. Chamberlain didn't deserve such joy in his life. He had interrupted the killer's enjoyment all those years ago and now the table would be turned.

He couldn't bear it any longer and he left his stake out and went home to plot further.

Meanwhile the two diners, oblivious of their audience and the angst they had caused, decided, as it was a Friday night, that they should go on for an after dinner drink somewhere that might have music.

They had established, during the conversation, that their musical tastes were probably not aligned very closely. He had admitted to the prog rock thing and after she had stopped laughing, she had said she was into disco and a bit of drum and bass. He had looked crestfallen but she laughed it off and said she would listen to anything really.

They went to a wine bar that had karaoke on so they just had a couple of drinks and listened to some appalling singing. They both laughed.

When it was time to go she asked him "So, Inspector Chamberlain, how do you think that went?"

"Oh I'll ask DCI Flemming in the morning. She is bound to fill me in" he said seriously. He knew that Judith would report every detail of their night out together and wouldn't hold back if he had messed up. His boss, in turn, would have no qualms about informing him about his failures. In fact she would enjoy it.

They went their separate ways, Chamberlain

puffing on his pipe and Judith Webster thinking about this rather moody, cynical but also entertaining policeman. She got her phone out of her bag and dialled her friends mobile number.

Chamberlain got home and went to sit in his armchair. He swapped to his 'home' pipe and just sat for a while wondering about this journalist women. Was she just being nice to him so she could get close to the case? They hadn't discussed it at all over the course of the night. It had been refreshing to be able to park his work for a while and just be normal, whatever that meant.

He heard the front door from downstairs shut. *She's late in, those bridge nights must go on a bit* he thought. Then his eye lids grew heavy, he rested the pipe on his knee and he fell asleep. He awoke with a start, looked at his watch and noticed it was 2.35am. He raised himself out of the chair and went upstairs to bed. He would probably feel like shit, having had a broken nights sleep.

# CHAPTER 30

The closing of the front door in the flat below DI Chamberlains house was not Mrs. Frobisher returning late from her Bridge night. It wasn't the right night for a start. No, it was an intruder.

Mrs Frobisher heard nothing. She was a good sleeper, always had been. She didn't hear the front door, not the footsteps along the hallway, nor the creak of her bedroom door.

This intruder was not a burglar. They had come prepared with some cable ties, a piece of cloth and some chloroform. The sole intention of the intrusion was to take Mrs. Frobisher from right under DI Chamberlain's nose. He wouldn't kill her there but would take her to his favourite place to do the deed. The path through the woods.

The shadowy figure crept around the basement flat and noticed the stairs leading up to the main house. He went up them, careful not to tread on any squeaky boards. At the top he noticed a dim light in one of the rooms and the smell of pipe smoke in the air. He crept forward, to a point where he could see through the door.

There was Chamberlain, asleep in an armchair,

with a smouldering pipe resting on his leg. Above the mantelpiece there was an impressive painting. *Interesting*, thought the intruder to himself. He crept back down the stairs to concentrate on the real point of his visit.

The extraction had gone surprisingly well, and quietly. She had been asleep and hadn't woken on the application of the chloroform soaked cloth. Her breathing had slowed and her body completely relaxed so he knew she was under.

She was slight of figure and he was a pretty strong man so carrying her up to street level and putting her in the boot of his car had been easy. No one had seen or heard him.

He then drove slowly and quietly away from Chamberlain's house and navigated his way out towards the Old Birmingham Road. There was no real expression on his face and he was feeling no sense of elation or anything else. This was just a mission that had to be completed. He didn't know the woman, had no feelings about her at all. He didn't care about her. She was a means to an end. Hopefully Chamberlain's end, eventually.

He didn't go to where the police had parked to access the path. No, he knew another access point that was not so obvious. He drove past the first lay-by and continued up the main road. After a while there was a narrow track leading up the outer edge of the woods in which he had watched his two poacher victims. It was an old farm track that led up around the top of the woods to a gate that led into the field where

Chamberlain and Harris had arrived at after their walk in the woods, up the path. His path.

He stopped at the gate and switched off the engine. It was deathly quiet. No noise from the boot of the car either. He gathered what he needed from the back seat and got out of the car, moving towards the rear.

The woman was still unconscious. Ok, easier to handle. He lifted her out and slung her over his shoulder. Then he made his way along the side of the field until he reached a stile. This lento a path. The other end of the path that had been the scene of the poachers demise.

He didn't go all the way to that scene but stopped in a semi clearing where there were several mounds. He knew these of old from when he had played in these woods as a child. They were now suiting his purposes very well. This wasn't the first time he had been here in the last few months.

There was a groan from the woman as he set her down on one of the mounds. It looked like she might be coming round now. He had better move quickly with the rest of the plan.

He put the snare around her neck and pulled it tighter and tighter. All he had to do next was to drive the peg into her shoulder.

# CHAPTER 31

DI Chamberlain went into the office in the morning. He hadn't had any breakfast, or coffee, so wasn't in a great mood. As he was passing his boss's office she called out to him. He stopped and went back as bidden.

"Ok, let me have it. Tell me all the things I did wrong last night. I know she will have rung you.' He said before Flemming could speak.

"I'm not your mother or a match maker you know" she said indignantly.

"She did ring you though, right?" He pressed.

"Well, maybe. But she swore me to secrecy so you will have to find out for yourself....Oh Romeo, oh Romeo..." she started, and then laughed.

"There is now very little of the aforementioned respect in your pot DCI Flemming" said Chamberlain. He didn't even bother to tell her to piss off.

"Just don't hurt her Ralph, she is my friend and I might have to kill you if you did." she said, protectively.

Chamberlain grunted. "I have been seeing a few of your friends recently."

"Ah yes. How did you get on with the Professor?" asked Flemming.

"Yeah, ok. I still think it was a little premature to be thinking we have 'a looney killer' as your friend put it. However, I do feel forewarned and forearmed if we do" said Chamberlain.

"Sounds like Richard. Anything else come out of any enquiries?" asked the DCI.

"I'm going along for a catch up after we finish here. I was expecting a dressing down, vicariously, about last night but as that isn't happening I'll get along there now." said Chamberlain with some relief.

His DCI simply smiled as he left her office. Judith had rung her, straight after the meal, and had gone into some detail about her impression of Detective Inspector Ralph Chamberlain. It had all been positive. She'd sounded like an excited schoolgirl.

Chamberlain arrived at the incident room. His team had heads down, getting on with their allotted tasks. He knew they would have been on to him if there had been any developments so he went straight through to his office. He had just sat down when DC Dixon knocked at the door and came straight in.

"Boss, message from the front desk" said

Dixon. "An anonymous caller just rang in and said to give you a message. 'Tell DI Chamberlain he is being a bit slow but maybe this one will chivvy him along a bit'. And that was it. They are trying to trace the call now".

"What the hell does that mean" Chamberlain said, more to himself than anyone else.

Dixon merely shrugged. There was some commotion out in the incident room. DS Harris rushed across and pushed past Dixon.

"Sir, another body has been found. Up the same path as the other ones. The cadaver dog team were on their way up there to start on those mounds we found when they came across it. It's female apparently but other than that, no further information."

"Shit" said Chamberlain. "Ok Tom, let's go and see what we have".

As they made their way back over to the Old Birmingham Road, Chamberlains imagination started to play havoc with him. Female, personal to him, if the phone call was connected. *Oh god, not Judith* his brain screamed internally.

There are no bounds to the human imagination. We are fed fantasy, and horror, from a very early age. It seems to be a parental duty to scare the living shit out of their children, literally sometimes. The Bogey Man, in the cupboard, the monster, under the bed.

Society and culture and the arts then nurture these horrors and develop them through films and books etc. Chamberlain's imagination was going double speed. What the hell was going on? If Judith was hurt, or dead, it would be his fault.

They arrived at the usual lay-by and left the car at speed and rushed up the pathway. It was pretty clear now after all the recent foot traffic. At the back of his mind Chamberlain wondered why he hadn't seen the dog vans and other police cars at the parking spot.

They were all there when they arrived at the scene. There was a forensic tent already covering the victims body.

"There's another way up here you know Inspector" it was Richard Bewley, the senior CSI. "Quicker too" he added.

"Really. Where?" Queried Chamberlain.

"You go a bit further up the main road and there is a narrow farm track that lead up the other side of that stretch of woods beyond that first field. You go through a gate and along the edge of the field. It leads to the other end of the path, just up through there." He pointed in the opposite direction from which Chamberlain and Harris had arrived.

"That's interesting. We will take a look in a bit. What have you got Richard" asked Chamberlain.

"Same MO, with the snare that is. Female this

time. Do you want to have a look?" Asked Bewley.

"Not really but I guess I have to" replied Chamberlain. He had seen a lot of dead bodies but it was never a pleasure. He approached the tent and started to enter. He stopped dead in his tracks and made a guttural, animal noise. There on the ground was his housekeeper, Mrs Frobisher, dead. She had a wire snare around her neck and the peg at one end had been driven into her shoulder.

"Oh, christ. It's my housekeeper" whispered Chamberlain, clearly in shock.

He retreated out of the tent and sat down heavily on a fallen tree trunk. He had turned a whiter shade of pale. Harris, Bewley and the others within earshot all stared at him in disbelief.

Harris was the first to speak. "Sir, are you absolutely sure?" He questioned. People could look different in death and Chamberlain had only had a glimpse of the body.

"Yes, I'm sure" said Chamberlain quietly.

He didn't know what to do. Normally, in these situations, he would get into scene of crime mode automatically and start an investigation. This time he was lost. He knew the victim. Sweet Mrs Frobisher, dear Mrs Frobisher. His anger started to rise from his core. This was personal. Someone was targeting him, or more to the point, people close to him. *Bastard.*

# CHAPTER 32

Back at the station, Chamberlain was sat in his DCIs office, staring at the floor. His mind was racing but there were no lucid thoughts arising from the activity. Stupid things occurred to him. What was her Bridge club going to do without her?

"Right." Said Flemming efficiently. "I'm not going to shut you out of the case Ralph but you are going to have to step back. You are not only in shock but you are also presumably in danger if this is all targeted at you. Bearing in mind the phone message, I think it is safe to assume it is."

The words sort of filtered through to Chamberlain and he knew she was right. But he certainly wouldn't drop it altogether. He was going to get this bastard, whoever it was. At the moment, he had no idea about who he might have pissed off enough to go to all this trouble.

"Ahhh Rebecca, what the fuck? Pardon my French but...." Chamberlain's words faded away.

"I know. I'm so sorry Ralph. From what you have told me in the past, I doubt the poor women had done anyone any harm in her life." Consoled Flemming.

"I hear what you say about being involved in the case but I can't just sit on the sidelines, I just can't" pleaded Chamberlain. "This is obviously directed at me so I am going to have to work out why. If this is some kind of vendetta, a macabre game, what have I done that has so upset someone they are prepared to kill, more than once, to get my attention? Why not just go after me?" Chamberlain was thinking aloud now.

"I can't answer these questions at the moment Ralph but we will get all available resources onto it, I can assure you." This, Chamberlain believed. Whenever one of their own was threatened or hurt, the whole force felt it and pulled together.

He needed air, space, his pipe.

"I'm going back to the scene to have a proper look around" he announced.

"Take Harris with you. That's an order not a suggestion." Said Flemming. She wasn't happy about him being exposed but at least if Harris was with him, he could watch his back. DS Harris was a good, reliable member of the team and she knew that he respected Chamberlain enormously and would throw himself in front of the proverbial bullet for him. At least, she hoped it was proverbial.

Chamberlain left her office without saying

another word. He was already going through a mental list of people he had brought down over his career. It had to be one of them, surely? He hadn't scorned any women...well not since he was a teenager. He hadn't upset any neighbours or friends....what about colleagues in the force? Unlikely but not impossible. Had he trodden on toes to get where he was today? He didn't think so, particularly.

No, it must be soon from an old case that he had caused to go to prison. Well, they had caused it really, he had just brought them to justice. He didn't think he had been involved in any miscarriages.

All these thoughts were rushing around in a whirlpool in his head. He found himself in the car park, and made for his cr. DS Harris was already sending by the vehicle.

"DCI Flemming told me not to let you out of my sight, Sir" Harris explained.

"Yes, thank you, good show" replied Chamberlain. He was very fond of Harris. A good young copper who he was sure was going to get better and better with experience. They both got into Chamberlains car.

"Where are we off to Sir?" Asked the younger man.

"Back to the scene, or should I say scenes of crimes Tom. Apparently there is another way to get to that top end of the path. You know, where we went the other day and found another field." He answered.

If the mounds they had seen turned out to be other bodies, they definitely had a serial killer. The odds of those killings not being committed by the same person as the latest ones were, in his view, impossible. It looked like they did have a 'looney killer' as per the Professors flippant remark. Chamberlain made a mental note to have another conversation with the academic at the earliest possible time.

Usual protocols out of the window for the present, Chamberlain was puffing away at his pipe whilst at the wheel. Trousers be damned…and the seat of the car. Another petty thought came into his head. Who was going to mend his burnt trouser pockets? Not for the first time, he started to doubt himself.

They sped past the usual parking spot and searched for the farm track. There it was, not obvious unless you were looking for it. They drove slowly up the rough surface until they got to a gate to a field, They stopped and got out.

"Our killer could have come this way, hidden in the woods this side of the field the cows were in and attacked from there" said Chamberlain. The cows would have obliterated any tracks he had left crossing that field. *Why had he not tried to disguise the depression from where he had spied on his victims?*

"You can't see this gate from the road so any vehicle would not have been spotted" said Harris.

There were vehicle tracks and ruts near the

SIMON FORD

gate but they were pretty much messed up by tractor traffic and the recent SOCO vans.

"He could have returned to here either from the top of the path and along to this gate, or back across the field and through the woods past his original hiding place....or I suppose he could have gone down the path back to the main road and walked up here to his vehicle. Risky though, going on the main road" said Chamberlain.

"Might have been ok in the middle of the night" said Harris. "Probably not much traffic at that time of the night" responded Harris.

They were ping-ponging ideas at each other.Harris's phone went. He listened for a while and then rang off.

"Apparently the cadaver dogs have been no good. They are too distracted by the scent of the recent body on the surface. They are going to have to get an archaeology team in to dig these mounds up and see what's there" he said to his boss.

"Right" said Chamberlain. He wondered if that had been deliberate on the part of the killer to delay their investigation. That didn't really make any sense as so far he seemed to be trying to speed things up.

He was assuming the killer was male but he supposed he shouldn't assume anything. Another chat with the Professor was getting more urgent.

"Let's walk round the top and approach down from the top end of the path" he instructed. Then stopped and had obviously re-though the plan. "On second thoughts, you go through the woods and across the field to the original scene of crime and I'll go along the top route".

They parted and went their allotted ways. Harris scrambled through the first part of the woods but then it got easier. He soon came across the indent in the ground that his boss had described to him earlier. It was obvious someone had lain there, the earth was compacted and the leaves swept to the side.

It felt eerie on his own in the woods. *Ridiculous* he thought to himself. *Get a grip Harris.*

There was a slight breeze and the beaches and leaves of the trees were rustling, as if whispering to him. He moved forward to the edge of the woods and looked across the field. Cows. They were docile, right? He stepped into the field and walked across towards the original crime scene. He wasn't sure how this was helping but you never knew with these things. *Build a picture* his boss would say.

Meanwhile, his boss was making his way along the top edge of the same woods, through a field, towards the top end of the path. Pipe lit, a haze following behind him. It looks like the field had been recently ploughed and the ruts were hard, making the going quite tough.

Eventually, he reached the stile that marked this end of the path. He climbed over it and started to walk down towards the spot where they had found Mrs Frobisher. He started to think about the woman he had known for over 4 years.

Mrs Frobisher had been recommend as a cleaner and initially had lived elsewhere and just visited on a couple of days a week to do the chores. She was very good and as Chamberlain got to know her better he decided to offer her the flat in the basement. It was just being used for storage and didn't take much to make it habitable. She had jumped at the chance.

She was very pleasant and unobtrusive. It also became apparent that she loved working in the garden. This was music to Chamberlain's ears. He had never had green fingers. Over the years, she had done more and more for him, including mending the burns in his trouser pockets. She was invaluable. Now she was gone. No, she didn't deserve this.

He reached the clearing with the mounds where her frail body had been discovered, by the farmer again. It was a lonely and remote place to die, and to be left, discarded, like some old rubbish. Whoever had done this was sick in the head. He, DI Chamberlain, vowed to seek them out and bring the force of the law down on them.

He looked around the area, studying the mounds. Some had a few tufts of grass on them but others seemed to be bare. Not much would grow under the canopy of leaves in this part of the woods. He doubted many people knew the area. The path appeared little used. Probably mostly used by foxes, badgers and other wild animals. Someone had chosen the place deliberately. He wondered how the farmer had come across the body.

He saw Harris arriving from the opposite direction.

"Right, back to the office and let's catch up with the team" said Chamberlain. There was little they could do until the mounds were investigated.

# CHAPTER 33

The killer was pretty pleased with himself. That would wake Chamberlain and his team up. The game was on. He could sit back and relax for a while. He still had some cash left over from the racecourse, enough to live on for the time being. He would have to be a little frugal, no more fancy hotels or fine dining for the moment.

He didn't see why he shouldn't enjoy some of these things from time to time. During his upbringing, his parents certainly hadn't treated him to anything.

"If you want things in life, boy, you have to earn them and get them yourself" his father used to say to him.

Well, he was doing that. His way might not be conventional but so what. And if people got in his way, then they had better watch out. Like DI Chamberlain. He had got in the way all those years ago and now, he had better watch out.

It hadn't just been the fact that the policeman had interrupted his kill. That was bad enough. But the consequences had gone further. That night he was put in such a bad mood that he had gone home, got in a huge argument with his foster parents and they had thrown him out. He then lost his job as he was sleeping rough and kept being late for work, unwashed and bedraggled. He blamed all of this on Chamberlain.

He had learned a lot of skills while he lived on the streets. How to blend in and go unnoticed, how to steal to survive, how to defend himself. It was a hard life and he had no desire to return to it now.

He stopped reminiscing. That was the past. He had a major project to keep him busy at the moment. He decided he needed to know more about this journalist, Judith Webster. If Chamberlain was getting close to her then she could be another lever, another thing personal to Chamberlain that would hurt him if she came to harm. He would spend a day shadowing her. She would have no idea, he was very good at being nobody. Everyone had always told him he would be a nobody. Not quite what they had meant maybe.

He started to think of ways to bring the project to a head. He envisaged luring Chamberlain somewhere and making him watch as he killed this woman in front of him, before killing the man himself. They say revenge is sweet. He hoped it would be.

Like DI Chamberlain, he was a lover of music. Unlike Chamberlain, his tastes were darker and certainly not 70s prog rock. No, he liked the moody, challenging, massive soundscapes produced by Gustav Mahler's works. He could sit and listed to them for hours. They went on for hours. It was time for a bit of Mahler's 5th Symphony, which he had on vinyl.

He had a fair amount of vinyl in his collection and he had a top quality Quad amp and pre-amp system that drove a pair of Tannoy speakers. He placed the record carefully on the Thorens turntable and set the music playing. Then he settled into the armchair and started to relax.

He knew a lot of people thought that the music of Mahler could be psychologically challenging. He didn't. He knew exactly what the man was on about through the compositions.

He preferred vinyl to the modern digital versions now so popular. You didn't get the peaks and troughs of the frequencies so smoothly and well defined in digital recordings. He listened on, drifting with the music. It was almost like flying if you closed your eyes.

Yes, his project was starting to go smoothly. DI Chamberlain was hooked in to the game and would be drawn further and further within his grasp until the final movement where he, the killer, the hero, would get his final satisfaction.

# CHAPTER 34

A meeting had been called for the incident room and as many as could make it were there. All the core team were present. DI Chamberlain and DCI Flemming were at the front of the room. Flemming had asked Chamberlain to lead the meeting.

"Good afternoon to you all" he began. "We need to step up on this. It appears to be personally linked to me so I should really step back. However, I don't intend to do so and DCI Flemming has agreed with me. If it is personal to me, then I am best positioned to try to work out the nitty gritty and find the basta… the perpetrator" he corrected himself.

There were murmurs and nods of agreement throughout the room. Protocol was all very well but he was right and they all understood.

"I will not make it obvious that I am still involved but rest assured I am beside you" he continued. "Now, any updates for us please?"

A couple of hands went up. They had obviously been working hard on the case behind the scenes. It wasn't the glamorous part of the job but essential and very often what got the eventual result.

"What have you got Dixon?" He picked the young DC first and she flushed slightly. He wanted to build her confidence in the team. He knew she was fastidious in her work but she needed to develop her team skills.

"Err, yes Sir. DC Norrish and I have been talking to as many people as we can in the pub, including the barman, although he was away for a couple of days so we had to go back this morning for him" she started to explain.

Chamberlain made a mental note of that. Where had he been, and doing what? It wasn't beyond the bounds of possibility that he wasn't involved and just happened to be away at the time Mrs Frobisher had been abducted and murdered. Despite what some people say, there are such things as coincidences in Chamberlain's opinion.

"Ok, come back to him if you don't mind. What about the other punters, particularly the group that included our first two victims?" He asked.

"There are a few of them and I think we spoke to most. The group is fluid and fluctuates from day to day. All the ones we spoke to appeared to be very shocked by what had happened and couldn't believe that Denton and Foxborough were capable of killing. They had all heard the discussion about the new poaching area that Denton had found but didn't think it was very serious although one of them, a Bob Simmons, said that Foxborough had muttered something about finding out where it was anyway. He thought he might have planned to follow Denton" she paused.

"Ok, well they were right, as it turns out weren't they" said DCI Flemming.

"There didn't seem to be anyone else we could find that had any idea what we were talking about. No one else appeared to know that group of drinkers and hadn't heard any arguments or even discussions about poaching." Dixon finished off.

"Ok, thank you Dixon" said Chamberlain. "Has anyone found any connection between the first two victims and Mrs. Frobisher?"

No one spoke. He knew that he and Mrs Frobisher were linked but he had no connection himself with the two poachers. They had no suspects and no real motive outside of some connection to him.

"What about forensics and pathology?" Chamberlain asked the room.

DS Harris spoke up, clearing his throat. "We have confirmation now that the snares used in the killing of Denton and Mrs Frobisher are exactly the same. It is safe to assume that our killer took one or more away from the initial scene. The MO is the same with the initial garrotting finished off by driving the peg into the rear of the victims shoulder, thus making it almost impossible to remove, at least in time for the victim to survive."

Chamberlain could only imagine the horror that poor Mrs Frobisher had gone through at the hands of this maniac.

"Unfortunately there doesn't appear to be any DNA that doesn't belong to the victim, in any of the three killings." Continued Harris.

"We appear to have a very efficient, forensically aware, killer on our hands" said DCI Flemming.

"Causes of death are the obvious in all cases" stated Harris.

As he appeared to have finished his contribution, DC Dixon put her hand up to indicate she was ready to report hers' and Norrish's findings. Chamberlain nodded at her to begin.

"We finally got to talk to the barman Rob Jones. He confirmed his earlier conversation with you sir, and added that he was not aware of any connection with the pub or the drinking group and Mrs Frobisher. He was a little loath to tell us where he had been for the last couple of days. We pressed him for the information and eventually he said he was seeing someone who lived the other side of Birmingham but they were married and he wanted to keep it on the down low. He did add, as a bit of an afterthought, that he seemed to remember a guy who used to sit at the end of the bar, near to where this group sit when they

THE WOODLAND PATH MURDERS

come in for their afterwork pints. He sat on his own and wasn't very talkative. Mr. Jones said he hadn't seen him for a few days" said Dixon.

"That's worth following up then" said Chamberlain. "He may have overheard the poacher's conversation. Does he have CCTV anywhere in the pub?"

"On a limited basis, at the front and rear entrances and one overlooking the bar area. He was going to get some footage sent over to us later today." Said Norrish.

"Ok, good work. Follow that up as soon as you can please" said Chamberlain. It was a long shot and would be too easy if they had their killer on video and easily identifiable, but you never knew.

"If this killer is really after me then I must have upset someone, most likely in a previous case. Maybe they got sent down because of me and are now out of prison and after revenge. I will make a list of possibles from old cases and start to eliminated them." Said Chamberlain. "I'm also going to talk to your friend Professor Phillips again. Let's see if he can spread any more light on the kind of person we are dealing with" he said, more to his DCI than the room as a whole.

"Dixon, you can help me with the old cases. The rest of you can study the CCTV footage when it arrives. M'am, can you get me another meeting with the professor please." On that he left the room. He already had his pipe in his hand and was headed for the car park.

"Just had a message come in from Cheltenham Sir" said Norrish. "They want know if we have had any luck finding their Racecourse thief".

"Tell them, no, we haven't. We are a bit busy with a serial killer at the moment" Chamberlain couldn't hide the sarcasm in his voice.

# CHAPTER 35

The grainy image from the racecourse had appeared on Crime Watch, the TV series aimed at enlisting the help of the public in catching criminals. The crime had been so brazen that they wanted to catch the thief before he tried the trick again, maybe not at Cheltenham, but at one of the many other racecourses in the country. One person who saw the story appear was Rob Jones, the barman. He had been preparing to open the pub and had the TV on in the bar.

"Bloody hell" he said out loud, though there was no one else in the pub. He stopped what he was doing and headed to the back office to make a phone call.

He got through to the desk sergeant at the police station and asked to speak to DI Chamberlain. After a short moment he was told that the DI was not in his office but if he left a message they would get him to contact Mr Jones as soon as possible. That would have to do for now he supposed

What he had seen might not be connected but he thought he should mention it to the Inspector. He carried on with his pre-opening routine and made a mental note to ask the fellas in the drinking group if they remembered the quiet bloke who sat at the bar.

The lunchtime session was quite busy so he had to put everything else out of his mind. He heard the phone in the office ring a couple of ties but was unable to get away from the bar to answer it. He had an answer phone and his usual policy was that if it was important they would either leave a message or ring again later.

Once the bar quieted down for the mid afternoon period, Rob Jones went back to the office and checked for messages. There was one. He played it. It was DI Chamberlain returning his call and it invited him to try and ring the police station again at his convenience.

He rang and was put straight through. "DI Chamberlain speaking, how can I help?" Said the voice.

"Yes...err...inspector, it's Rob Jones from the pub. I thought I should ring you. I've seen 'im....on the telly." Said Jones in a rush.

"You've seen who, Mr Jones?" Coaxed Chamberlain.

"The fella I told your lot about who used to sit at the bar and say nowt!" He said, calming down a bit. "He was on that Crime Watch programme about some theft at Cheltenham Racecourse. It was definitely him...thought you should know." Said Jones.

"Ok, thank you for that Mr Jones. Can you ring us immediately if you see him again, in the pub or elsewhere, please?" Said Chamberlain.

"Sure thing" said Jones.

They ended the call and Chamberlain went through to his team and tasked DC Norrish with getting the footage from the latest Crime Watch programme and checking the PNC for details of a theft at Cheltenham. The racecourse was out of their patch but that didn't necessarily mean this wasn't connected. Then again, it might not be.

"Let me know when you have all the info. This could be our first break. A lead, a suspect" said Chamberlain, enthusiastically.

He must now make a call to Professor Phillips who was unable to meet up but could spare a few minutes on the phone with him.

Just then, DS Harris waved him over and said. "I just heard back from the team up at the scene with the mounds. They have dug up one and there is a skeleton. The Forensic Archaeologist reckons it could be a couple of thousand years old so not a recent disposal. They will have to check each one to be sure the others are the same of course."

"Ok, well let's hope they are all like that" said Chamberlain. "I'll need to speak to the Archaeologist, can you get him to come in when he has a chance?"

He went back to his office to ring the Professor. He answered after two rings and said he would have to be quick as he was due elsewhere.

"I understand, and thank you for taking the time to speak to me. I guess Rebecca will have brought you up to date with events down here?" assumed Chamberlain.

"Yes, indeed she has" said the Professor. "It would appear she was right in the first instance about what you are dealing with. I would re-iterate the things I told you when we met, though you may not remember it all. The human brain has a way of sub-consciously remembering information that seems important at the time, not necessarily stuff we would dearly like to recall at a later date."

"I remember most of it I think Professor. It was only a couple of days ago. I would, however, like a little more detail about what sort of person we are likely to be dealing with here" asked Chamberlain.

"I don't have long enough to teach you everything DI Chamberlain. Do you have any specific questions?" said the Professor.

"Other than the obvious connection to me, why did he chose my housekeeper as a victim? Why not one of my team?" asked Chamberlain.

"Generally, serial killers select their victims based on certain physical and/or personal characteristics. When a serial killer begins their hunt for human prey, it is almost always true that they know absolutely nothing about the person who is to become their victim. Is there any correlation between the victims you have so far/ e.g. gender, background, physical type?"

"I suppose two of them were fairly slight and weak individuals" said Chamberlain, thinking of Denton and Mrs Frobisher.

"A psychopath will pick up on a whole suite of nonverbal cues, including the length of their stride, how they shift their weight, and how high they lift their feet. Taken together, these cues give the psychopathic men a rough gauge of how confident their potential victims are. Body language that implies a lack of confidence includes lack of eye contact, fidgeting of the hands and feet, and the avoidance of large gestures when shifting posture. Just as psychopaths are a special breed, so too are their victims." Continued Phillips.

"So you are saying this psychopath chose his victims because they were weaker than him? What about the connection to me? I have never heard of Denton and Foxborough" said Chamberlain.

"It's possible this killer has a preferred type and the first victims were simply to attract your attention. When you didn't initially bite, he had to find someone close to you i.e. your housekeeper. She was a small lady beyond middle age, whereas any of your team are presumably young in comparison, pretty fit and healthy and would not be easy to overpower." Said Phillips.

"Ok, if I accept all that, I now have to work out the 'why'" mused Chamberlain.

"I'm not sure I can help specifically with that but the kind of person you are looking for has probably had a bad, violent, unloving childhood, has grown up into a controlling, unforgiving, violent adult who has no empathy for other living things. He is therefore very dangerous." explained Phillips. "You should try to appreciate that our childhood references may include Blue Peter, Raleigh Chopper bicycles and Nesquik milk shakes. A psychopath's more likely include loneliness, abuse and pain".

"Well, mine would be Rubik's Cube and video games...still Blue Peter, obviously, but I understand what you mean" said Chamberlain. He wondered about his own upbringing. In many ways, an unremarkable childhood. Not terrible but not spectacular. Would people say 'a normal childhood'?

"Yes, sorry, I am a little older than you, Inspector!" Phillips said, smiling.

They finished their call as the Professor ran out of time. Chamberlain sat back in his chair and thought deeply and worryingly about this mysterious foe that had picked him as his adversary for an, as yet, unknown reason. Old case files next then.

# CHAPTER 36

DI Chamberlain spent the afternoon going through old files with the assistance of DC Dixon. She was very efficient at pulling the relevant details from the old cases. Despite this, they couldn't find anything that might lead them to a suspect. It was very frustrating and Chamberlain went out a couple of times for a puff on his pipe and the second time he came back with coffee and buns.

After lots more records they stopped again. It was getting late so they called it a day.

"Do you have someone waiting for you at home Dixon" asked Chamberlain, casually.

"Yes Sir, well, not at home exactly. I have a boyfriend but we don't live together. Not sure if that will happen or not to be honest." She stopped, realising she was going into more detail than the Inspector had really wanted.

"Hmmm" he murmured, "Tricky I expect, with long hours and so on." He added, to make her feel better.

It didn't really make her feel better. It just

highlighted the problems that she was having in her relationship. It wasn't that her fella didn't understand. It was just that they got to spend little time together, or little quality time. She loved her work, and she thought she loved him but sometimes it just seemed impossible to move forward with the relationship.

She had met Luke in a night club and they hit it off straight away. It was probably the drink's fault but they had gone back to his place and slept together that first night. The next day had been a Saturday and nether were working so they had spent the day together, walking around town, drinking coffee, having lunch in a little cafe. They had talked and talked, endlessly it seemed at the time. She had been upfront about her work and the hours it sometimes involved. He had said he could handle it.

Well, that was 7 months ago and they were still juggling work and play time and things just weren't quite right. He was a joiner and worked on building sites. In his spare time he made bespoke furniture. He was good and made a fair living at it.

Maybe she was making too much of it but something was itching at her and she didn't know what to do. The physical side of the relationship was great but she knew that sex alone wasn't the basis for a long term situation. She didn't know if she wanted all the things a girl was supposed to want...the perfect husband, the house, the children and all the trimmings but she knew what she had now was not enough. She would have to talk to Luke again and see what he really felt about them. She resolved to do that tonight…. as long as something urgent didn't come up with the current case.

Chamberlain had instructed all of his team be be extra vigilant and, if possible, not to travel alone. There was no guarantee that they would not be targets, despite what the Professor had said about victim profiles.

He suddenly thought about Judith. She wasn't really connected to him other than the fact they had dined together the other night. He should warn her anyway, whilst trying not to worry her too much. He didn't want to scare her but he didn't want her to be caught up in this if it could be avoided. He would ring her on the pretext of meeting up again to discuss doing another press release, possibly including a photograph of the Cheltenham thief.

She answered her phone promptly "Judith Webster"

"Hi Miss Webster, it's DI Chamberlain here. Can you talk?" he said, rather formally.

"Oh, hi Ralph" she said confidently, after all, they had dined together. She felt she could use his first name now. "What can I do for you?"

"Well, first of all, I wanted to thank you for your company the other night. I enjoyed it very much" he said. They had both thanked each other at the time but he was nothing if not a gentleman when it came to these things. An awkward, somewhat shy gentleman but one nonetheless. He had no idea what he was doing really. There was something about this woman that intrigued him. He was definitely attracted to her. What he couldn't work out was whether his thoughts were reciprocated. Was she just flirting to get access to him and the case? *Too cynical?* he thought to himself.

"Yeah, me too. Shall we do it again then?" She certainly appeared to have more confidence than he did.

"Well....err...yes, that would be nice" he stuttered. *That would be nice - very smooth.* "Actually Judith, I need to meet up asap to discuss another press release. Are you available for a coffee now?" He returned to a more formal footing, one he was comfortable with.

"Sure. Where do you want to meet?" She said, with a lightness in her tone that tugged at him again.

They agreed to meet at the cafe just round the corner from the police station and she said she could be there in 20 minutes. On his way there, Chamberlain reflected on his past history with the opposite sex. It was lamentable really. A few short term relationships in his teens followed by a very short marriage to a girl called Marie. She went to the same school as he did and they married too young, or maybe it was just they weren't really compatible. Whichever, it only last two years. He had joined the force and his focus was on that rather than the marriage. The relationship deteriorated and they eventually separated.

Since then, he had been married to the job. He didn't really get time to be lonely, or to meet suitable prospective partners. So what was it about this Judith Webster that had got his juices running again? *Grow up, Chamberlain* he told himself.

As soon as he entered the cafe and saw her sitting there, his resolve to grow up left swiftly through the open door and left him helpless, on his own, to deal with Judith Webster, the woman. She leapt up with a huge smile and greeted him.

"Hi, you" she said simply. Just those two words seemed to embrace an unspoken intimacy.

"Hello Judith. Thanks for coming" he started with. They ordered coffee and sat opposite each other. "Judith, before we talk about a press release, I need to warn you about something."

"Sounds serious" she frowned. He noticed she looked just as attractive when she frowned as when she smiled.

"It is, or could be. I don't want to alarm you but it would appear that this case is centred around me, some kind of vendetta. There has been another killing, similar MO, and it was my poor dear housekeeper, Mrs. Frobisher. Someone appears to be playing games with me. If this is true, then anyone who knows me could be at risk. I need you to be vigilant and just watch your back." He said seriously.

"Wow!" She exclaimed. "We only just met and

already my life is in danger?" Although he thought she may have been trying to make light of the situation, he could tell she was worried.

"I can only apologise. I wish I didn't have to frighten you like this but if we are right, then this person is very dangerous - psychopathic even." Continued Chamberlain. "Just be careful, don't travel alone at night, make sure your doors are locked …that kind of thing."

"Blimey, you are serious about this aren't you?" It was a rhetorical question.

Chamberlain moved on to the subject of the press release in an attempt to steer away from the initial conversation. They agreed that she would arrange for the photograph to appear in the paper the following day, without her name next to the article this time.

It went quiet for a few moments "And yes, I would love to have dinner with you again" had he said that out loud?

Her face brightened. "Ok, cool. Where and when?" she chirruped. Surely he wasn't imagining the enthusiasm in her response. What did worry him was whether he was drawing her nearer to danger by his pursuit of her on a personal basis.

# CHAPTER 37

"Shit!" The killer had just seen his own image splashed across the crime pages of the newspaper. He had been careless, reckless even. He read the accompanying copy and frowned. They were looking for him in connection with the theft, but also as a possible witness to a local incident. At least they didn't have a name for him. Talking of names, there was no attribution name to the story.

"Oh, don't be coy about your involvement, Miss Webster" he said to the empty room. "Your role is by no means over my dear".

It seemed they hadn't made a full connection to him and the murders but they were getting close. Good. He would have to enact the finale sooner rather than later before they found him, which no doubt they would.

Time for more Mahler. It was his form of meditation, calming his mind and body. Some of the orchestral movements matched his dark thoughts and sometimes he found he could drift away into fantasy, other times he could plan clearly for his project.

He started to get the necessary kit together which he would keep ready in a small backpack. His twisted version of a 'go bag'. There were thick, strong cable ties, a roll of gaffer tape, a large sharp kitchen knife, a 10m length of climbing rope, gloves and a balaclava. He checked them off a mental list as he placed them in the pack, imagining the scenario when they would be put to full and good use.

This job done he went to settle in the armchair for some more R&R. Yes, things were coming together nicely. The dips and swells of moody Mahler hung in the air. How was he going to execute the final act in his project? He needed a location, of course, but he also needed to catch the bait and then cast the line out to hook the ultimate prey.

He still had the chloroform from when he took Mrs Frobisher so it shouldn't be too difficult. He would stake out the bait prey and find out the best time and place to do it. Then it should be fairly easy to hook the main prey as he was pretty sure DI Chamberlain was very keen on Miss Webster and would leap to her defence. How heroic. Well, that would be his downfall.

He wasn't sure if Chamberlain had made the connection with him but no matter. Events didn't depend on that. He was hopeful that when face to face he would remember. The joyless smile returned to his face as he drifted off into a deep dreamless sleep.

This was rare for him. Sleep usually didn't come easily to him, a result of insufficient emotion regulation, manifesting in negative thoughts and behaviour, which affected his sleep quality. However, tonight, his mind seemed to be relaxed and somewhat content, perhaps because his plan appeared to be coming together.

# CHAPTER 38

The next morning in the incident room, DC Norrish was going through as much local CCTV as he could find to see if there was any footage of this mystery racecourse thief who just happened to be a caster in the same pub as the first two victims.

His phone rang and the desk sergeant said he had a call from some hotel manager about the photograph they had put in the newspaper.

"Good morning sir" he greeted. "How can I help you?"

"Yes, umm, I think the guy in the photo stayed at this hotel a few days ago. He was here for two nights and ate in the restaurant here. He was paying cash for everything." Said the man.

"Ok, sounds interesting. Do you have a name and address for the man?" Asked Norrish.

"Yes. A Mr. Ronald Denton from an address in Warwick." He said, and rattled off the address.

Norrish sat bolt upright. That was the name and address of the poacher. He was dead so it couldn't have been him. It must be the killer, the cheeky bastard. He thanked the man and ended the call. Then he rushed over to Chamberlains office and relayed the conversation to his boss.

"This could be our murderer *and* the racecourse thief" said Chamberlain. They had a face though not a real identity but it was a start. They were closing in. Perhaps their killer was getting over confident and would make more mistakes. He just hoped he wouldn't kill anyone else before they caught him.

"Have we heard anymore from the forensic archaeologist digging up those mounds?" He asked.

"I'll chase them up sir" said Norrish.

"And where is DS Harris this morning?" Chamberlain hadn't seen him yet this morning.

"I think he has gone back to the pub to speak to the barman, Rob Jones again. He said something didn't add up though he wasn't sure what yet." Said Norrish.

"Ok" said Chamberlain. He was intrigued. What had his sergeant found that he hadn't wanted to tell him about yet. "You carry on with the CCTV footage please"

DC Dixon was getting coffee and then they were going to finish off going through the last few relevant files. He didn't hold out any hope but it had to be done.

Coffee and buns arrived just as DC Norrish got off the phone to forensics. He went over to his boss's office.

"Just spoken to forensics, Sir. They have excavated two more of the mounds and they both contain very old remains. Same age as the first one roughly. They are continuing and will let us know any developments" he said.

"Thanks Norrish" said Chamberlain. It was looking like they just had an old burial site and not a modern disposal. It was a good thing but wouldn't help their case.

About an hour later, DS Harris walked back in to the incident room and went straight over to his boss's office in the corner.

"Ah, Tom. Anything for us" asked Chamberlain.

"Yes, sorry to be mysterious but I had a hunch but wanted to check first before mentioning it" he started, "I spoke to Rob Jones, the barman, again and he told me that he remembered one occasion where the mystery guy at the bar did engage in conversation with Ronald Denton at the bar once a couple of weeks ago. He thinks they were looking at a map. It could be that he gave Denton the information about this new area to go poaching for rabbits. Ergo, he set the trap for him and knew where he would be."

"So are you saying that our killer already knew the path up through those woods and effectively lured the man there?" Asked Chamberlain.

"I think it is possible sir, yes" replied Harris.

"Good work, Tom. What put you onto it in the first place?" Chamberlain asked.

"Well, it was never apparent why Denton went there. He said to the group that he had learned about a new area good for rabbits so someone must have told him. These things usually happen in pubs. Great place to do business, they say" explained Harris.

"Or choose your victim" said Chamberlain. "And having been rebuffed by Denton, Foxborough decides to follow him and discover this new hunting ground" he surmised.

"Makes sense" said Harris.

"Sir!" Came a call from the other side of the room. It was Norrish. He rushed over. "Forensics have started on the fourth mound and the earth is much looser apparently. They think this one must be more recent. They have paused in case you want to be there when they carry on digging"

"Tom, with me" said Chamberlain. "Tell them we re on our way".

Chamberlain blue lighted the journey and didn't hang around. They got to the parking spot in record time and hurried up the path. There were white suited SOCOs standing around waiting for them. One of the suits approached them.

"Inspector Chamberlain? I am Bill Archer, forensic archaeologist" said the suit. "Thanks for getting here so quickly." Tom looked at his boss and raised his eyebrows. He wasn't keen on his boss's fast diving skills.

"Hi, what have we got?" Asked Chamberlain.

"Well, the ground is much softer than the other mounds, indicating it has been disturbed much more recently. We haven't gone any further as we were waiting for you. We'll get on with it now you are here." Said Archer.

They got going again on the mound. It was painstakingly slow work. They knew they had to be careful not to disturb any potential forensic evidence. Chamberlain wandered away from the scene and retrieved his pipe from his pocket. Every time he did so now, it reminded him of poor Mrs Frobisher. He became very sad all of a sudden. He drew heavily on the pipe and the hot smoke burnt his tongue slightly.

He looked though the trees and into the field. No cows but what looked like the farmer was standing staring across in his direction. He turned away, and walked back to where the action was going on.

After about 45 minutes a call came up from one of the diggers. It sounded like they had found something. The white suit stood up and was holding a piece of material. It was dirty with the mud but you could still see the colour of it, a pale blue. It also had a pattern on it. Paisley. They didn't have that 2,000 years ago. They continued the excavation.

"We have a body Sir." Came a voice. "It's not fully decomposed so it's not like the others".

"Ok everybody, stop there. I think we have to treat this as a crime scene now. Wouldn't you say, Inspector?" said Archer

"Yes" came the sad reply. "Yes, we do. Mr Archer, what's the story here do you think? We seem to have a mix of old and modern burials. Why do you think the killer chose here as his disposal site?"

"Where to start, Inspector" said Archer. "This woodland is probably pretty old but may not be contemporary with the original mounds. There is quite a lot of Iron Age history in this area, some we know about, some still to discover. This may be part of the latter. Have you heard of Tocil Wood, up near Warwick University?"

"Can't say I have, to be honest" replied Chamberlain.

"It's just off Gibbet Hill Road and is now a Nature Reserve. Gibbet Hill Road represents the probable continuation of the prehistoric Hollow Way, which runs from Westwood past Brickyard Plantation. Within Tocil Wood, close by the road, is the site of a small, defended rectilinear, or rectangular, Iron Age enclosure. Nearby we have found mounds similar to these which probably date to the same time. These mounds here may originally be connected to another Iron Age settlement or fortification that was here before the woods developed" explained Archer. "It's quite exciting, apart from the modern burial and the murdered lady of course".

"Right, so did the murderer just chose this place by chance, do you think?" asked Chamberlain. "Or is this area already known about?"

"No, this is completely new for us. And as for why the murderer chose it, I couldn't say. That's for you lot to find out I would suggest. The trees here are clearly quite old but if you want to know more about the history of this woodland and forests in general, I would recommend you speak to someone at the Royal Forestry Society" said Archer.

"Ok, well, thank you for the information. Please keep us updated with your progress here" concluded Chamberlain. He wandered off to find Harris.

He was thinking that it couldn't be co-incidence that the killer had chosen this spot. He must have had prior knowledge and tried to use the old burial mounds to hide his activities. Why then the change in MO, leaving his recent kills above ground to be easily found?

# CHAPTER 39

Back at the police station there was much activity. The body had been established as male and the clothing was contemporary, modern day. They had found a wallet with ID which named the body as 35 year old Simon Whittall, from an address in Warwick. They would have to wait for final confirmation from DNA or dental records as the face was unrecognisable.

The forensic archaeologist reckoned the body had been in the ground no more than about 6 months. Although Chamberlain knew that coincidences did happen, the chances of this being a different killer were very small indeed.

They would, of course, have to try to link the killings and that might take some time. But for now, Chamberlain was convinced they were the same perpetrator. A serial killer. He wondered if any of the other mounds, as yet un-investigated, also held such a secret. There were four more.

Pathology were doing the autopsy and Professor Reed had promised to get on with it as fast as hc could.

Some of the team were trawling through more

CCTV footage.

DI Chamberlain was sitting in his office with his boss, DCI Flemming, sitting opposite him.

"I don't think we can avoid the fact that we probably have a serial killer on our patch. When this gets out, and it will, there will be panic in the population" said Flemming. "Can we continue to get help from Judith on this do you think?".

"I don't know M'am. I didn't want to involve her any more than necessary. If the killer is after me, he might see her as a target. I've told her to be vigilant but she is not used to this sort of thing." said Chamberlain.

"You like her, don't you Ralph?" quizzed Flemming.

"That's beside the point" he said gruffly. "Our job is to protect the public, whoever they are" he added.

"Ok, ok" she said, holding her hands up. She knew Judith liked him. They had had a long conversation the previous evening. She had known Judith long enough to know she wasn't frivolous with her romantic notions. If she said she liked Ralph Chamberlain then she really liked him.

"Sorry" he said. "It's just bad timing I guess. Long term relationships are hard work, they take compromise, mutual respect, managing expectations and most of all friendship, not just physical attraction.

At the moment, I need to be able to concentrate on catching this bastard. Yes, she is lovely. And I don't doubt you will feed back my comments to her but she needs to know how seriously dangerous this could be"

"Fair comment. I'll reiterate your warnings about watching her back" said Flemming. "So how are we going to catch this bastard, as you call him?"

"We do what we always do. We follow every lead, study the forensics, speak to people, and of course hope for a huge dollop of luck." said Chamberlain.

DCI Flemming left his office having agreed the course of action. Ralph Chamberlain, the man, let his thoughts drift to Judith Webster. It had been a long time since he had had similar feelings....any feelings if he was honest... for a woman. Was he ready for this? He didn't want to hurt her, or himself for that matter. He had a massive fear of rejection....together with as big a fear of missing out. *I'm an idiot* he told himself.

Snapping back to reality, he wanted to know more about this latest victim. Family, place of work, friends, enemies etc. He instructed the team to go ahead and do the usual enquiries.

And then, there could be more bodies waiting for them in the other mounds. It would be a while until they had finished with the current one so he would have to be patient on that score. In the meantime, full speed ahead on what they had so far.

He rang Judith and arranged to have dinner

with her the following evening. His DCI was right. They needed the help of the media on this. That was his excuse anyway. He knew he didn't actually need to meet her himself re the press release but his boss seemed to be happy to leave it to him to liaise with her friend. Was there some sort of female conspiracy going on here? Probably. The eternal battle of the sexes. He didn't consider himself sexist, or a misogynist by any means but there did seem to be a code, an unknown language, between the females of the species. His opinion was 'Vive la difference' as the French would say.

Chamberlain realised this may not be viewed as a particularly 'woke' standpoint but he was still going through the process of learning what the concept meant. It seemed to him that each new generation would come up with new words and ideas, sometimes in automatic rebellion against the older generation. Not that that was a bad thing of course. It just made it hard to keep up sometimes.

Back in her office, DCI Flemming reflected on the recent events, not only with regard to the case but also with her friends and the team she had under her. Were things developing between Chamberlain and her friend Judith Webster? If so, was it healthy? She cared about both of them.

She had worked hard to get where she was, not least because she was a woman. She would never use that as an excuse but you couldn't escape the fact that even nowadays there was an imbalance between the sexes in terms of opportunities and the way individuals were treated.

Her mixed race heritage, and hence her darker skin, and the fact she was a woman hadn't slowed her career progression so far but she was unsure where the glass ceiling might be. She wasn't bitter about it. She was pragmatic. That was the way of the world however much you disliked it. She didn't want to be favoured as a token either. She just knew she could do the job.

She was very grateful for the breaks life had given her. She had built a reputation, and now a team, of which she was proud. She didn't want anything to spoil or change that. She was also very fond of her friend and didn't want to see her hurt. Maybe she was being too sensitive and over-worrying about it but then, that was her job, to look after her team and it was a friend's job to watch out for those they cared about.

Then she thought about her own situation and immediate future, if she had one. She had recently felt a lump in her breast and had visited a doctor. She was now waiting for the result of a biopsy. She hadn't told anyone about this. No point until she knew one way or the other.

Meanwhile, DI Chamberlain had taken the Archaeologists advice and was on the phone to someone at the Royal Forestry Society. They seemed quite excited to be helping the police with their enquiries though Chamberlain hadn't gone into too much detail about the location and nature of the case.

"So, are you saying that the woods around there are relatively new?" asked Chamberlain.

"Well, yes and no" came the reply. "It is likely that the area was fully covered in forest after the last ice age, some 10 - 12,000 years ago. Sometimes referred to as the 'wildwood'. Then man came along and started using trees as a resource, for building and burning etc. With agriculture there would have been large areas cleared for farming. Vast amounts of forest would have been lost to these activities, but it would have been patchy."

"Ok, all fascinating" said Chamberlain. "But what about more recently".

"Well, the Romans brought greater infrastructure to Britain, and agriculture greatly expanded. Woodland cover was reduced and became much more managed to supply the wood and timber that supported the Roman settlements and industries" said the forestry boffin. "What I saying, in short, is that it is very difficult to know what is original woodland and what is relatively new. It is possible that the area of which you speak has a varied history of woodland, farmland, settlement, fortification, at various times of its' history. Perhaps not very helpful but without going there and doing in depth research I can't really say more than that".

"Ok, but if, for example, there were burial mounds in the woodland, they may precede the current tree growth?" suggested Chamberlain.

"Oh absolutely" said the boffin. "Of course, during Tudor times when the British navy expanded hugely to cope with the threat of invading foreign forces, the demand for timber was massive. It is calculated that to build one galleon, they needed around 2,000 trees! If you multiply that by the estimated number of ships that went up against the Spanish Armada, some 100 or so, that adds up to a lot of trees. At one point the fleet consisted of around 200 ships. The Oak tree population was decimated."

"I'm afraid I couldn't tell you what trees go to make up the woods in question but they aren't pine, for sure. They look reasonably old but I am no expert" said Chamberlain.

"Well, if there was an ancient settlement or such, in that location, the farming may have avoided it and new woodland may have grown up around it." explained the boffin.

"Ok, well, thank you so much for your time. You have been very helpful" Chamberlain ended the call.

Chamberlain wasn't quite sure whether all the information given by the boffin helped the investigation or not but it could be part of the story. Very interesting as well.

# CHAPTER 40

Meanwhile, the enquiries were continuing into the discovery of the body in the mound. Also, further mounds were now being investigated. So far, one more 2,000 year old skeleton had been found.

Looking into family, friends and work place of the latest body, some interesting facts had emerged. It turned out that Simon Wittall had been missing for about 3 months. It had been on the system but without any further information the story had gone luke warm.

There were no problems at home or as far as they could establish with friends. However, when they spoke to Wittall's work colleagues, it transpired that another, now ex, employee and Wittall had had a big fall out over something at work.

The work in question was a small manufacturing business on an estate in the suburbs of South Birmingham. They made plastic extrusion products of all shapes and sizes. Wittall had been promoted over this other guy who was not happy about it. He had been there longer than Wittall and felt the position should have been his.

This disgruntled employee had left the job in

THE WOODLAND PATH MURDERS

a huff, quite some time before Wittall went missing so no connection was made at the time. With the discovery of his body, everything was looked at again and in more detail. This ex-employee had a name and address.

Charles Hopgood, from an address in Redditch.

Officers had been despatched to the address but had found it empty and apparently un-lived in for some time. Forensics were there going over the property with a fine toothed comb. Chamberlain wasn't expecting any great results but it had to be done.

So, they had a potential suspect, if only they could find him. All the usual sources, DVLA, Electoral Roll, had him listed at the empty address. No apparent criminal record either. Not very helpful to their enquiry.

They had hundreds of responses to the Crime Watch appearance and the following newspaper appeal. It was going to take forever to go through these for elimination. If they struck lucky, they might find a useful lead, but the chances were slim.

They had DNA samples from all of the victims, and now from this Charles Hopgood, from a coat he left behind at the job he had walked out on in such a hurry. None of it really got them anywhere until they had something to compare one of them with. And they couldn't do that until they caught up with this suspect. All of the members of the team were frustrated by the lack of progress.

Then they got a break, of sorts, because Charles

Hopgood turned up. Well, his body turned up in the next mound to be excavated. Although he was without a wallet with standard ID in it, he did have a letter in his inside jacket pocket addressed to Charles Hopgood, from a dentist.

It was then fairly straightforward to get the said Dentist to confirm the identity of the body from dental records.

So who was the fake Charles Hopgood? DI Chamberlain suspected that their serial killing psychopath had killed Hopgood at some point and taken a new job having assumed his identity. This meant that they had no idea of the killer's true identity. They were moving forward but not fast enough and the more they found, it seemed the more questions there were to answer.

In his office, Chamberlain was on the phone to his boss, DCI Flemming.

"I realise this is uncomfortable for the folks on the upper floors but we are doing our best down here." He pleaded.

DCI Flemming had been in meetings with her bosses and they had been pressing her for results so naturally she was passing the pressure down the line. Chamberlain happened to be the next recipient.

"I know, I know" she said with a big sigh. "But you know what they are like. They seem to have forgotten what happens in the real world of crime."

"This guy is after me for some reason. Dixon

and I have looked through all my old cases and can't find anything that matches up….unless it's something that didn't become a case, or is outside of my work in the police" he added as an afterthought.

"Something from your dark and mysterious past, you mean? said his boss.

"Well, I wouldn't have put it quite like that but…yes, maybe." said Chamberlain. "I need to go for walk in the fresh air and get the pipe billowing" he put the phone down without the courtesy of saying goodbye.

Once outside he lit his trusty pipe. He needed space to let his mind think back over the years. He wandered down towards the river. The noise of running water was always calming to him. Visually too, running water was a little like watching the flames of a camp fire. Mesmerising. Hypnotic.

He let his mind think back over the years. Before he joined CID there were probably hundreds of people he had thwarted in terms of police work. Mostly petty crime. There was the guy who said he had been attacked and was in a pretty bad way but Chamberlain had never seen the attacker, and as far as he was aware, neither had the attacker seen him, up close at least. The papers had made a bit of a thing about it….well, one possibility, but there was never any suspect so they couldn't chase that up.

Anyway, if this was a response to that, it was wholly disproportionate. No one had been caught let alone been charged, gone to court and spent time in prison. He dismissed it.

His personal life had not been particularly adventurous or dangerous. He thought back to his schooldays. He hadn't been a bully. Quite the opposite, he had stood up for those that had suffered bullying. It hadn't resulted in anyone being expelled or unduly punished as far as he could remember.

He decided, lovely as it was by the river, that he wasn't getting anywhere. Perhaps a wander around the town, listening to the hubbub of people getting on with their daily lives, might jog a memory.

He left the peaceful riverbank and headed into town.

# CHAPTER 41

The killer had been busy. He had wanted to find somewhere not too far away but quiet enough not to be disturbed when it came to the final act. He discovered that Warwick Castle was undergoing certain renovations following a bad fire. This meant that it was closed to the public. Ideal.

He had scoped the building all day and there didn't appear to be any works being carried out at the moment. They had probably run out of money. The layout of the Castle was such that it would take quite an effort to get his kidnap victim to the chosen spot if she was still out cold. He would probably have to wait until she was conscious and lead her on foot to his chosen stage.

To avoid detection he would have to do this part under cover of darkness. He could control when the other actor should enter the stage. If necessary, he would simply invite DI Chamberlain to join him at a specific time. He was in control, all the way.

He really did enjoy all of this. The planning, the execution and the feeling of elation after the fact. The only downside was that he wanted more of a thrill each time and the elation was of shorter duration. He would just have to do more. He appeared to be very good at it so not a real problem.

The current project was interesting as there was a cumulative end game. The downfall and ultimate death of DI Chamberlain. Other projects had been individual subjects with no connection to outside influences.

Talking of outside influences, it wasn't yet clear as to when or how he would 'acquire' Miss Webster. He would just have to keep observing and following her every move. He mustn't hurt her in the abduction at the risk of her dying too soon. This was critical in the execution of the plan. Chloroform. He still had some. He had stolen it from a pesticide company he had worked for for a short while. Primitive but effective. He had to be careful with its' application as too much could causes heart failure. He had researched it diligently. It wasn't used any more in medicine or cosmetics but it was still used in organic chemistry, dye making and agriculture.

No, he needed Miss Webster to be alive, at least until he had Chamberlain in his grasp. They would both end up dead but Chamberlain needed to see his friends death, in detail. He had no feelings about her. She was collateral damage as far as he was concerned. A means to an end.

In a way he was grateful to the two poachers he had killed. They had shown him a new way of killing. The snare garrotte. He had added his own twist by driving the peg into the back of the victim to stop them being able to loosen the noose. He was proud of that bit. Thinking on his feet as he did. Yes, he would continue with this method, at least for the time being. His MO, as people liked to call it.

# CHAPTER 42

As he meandered through the streets of Warwick, Chamberlain wondered if he was being watched. Any of the men he saw could be the killer they were hunting. Or even any of the women. It wasn't beyond the realms of possibility that the killer was female, or maybe even just disguised as such. He felt more like the hunted than the hunter at the moment.

He found himself outside Rob Jones's pub. *May as well go in*. He went in and sauntered up to the bar. Rob was cleaning glasses behind the bar.

"Inspector. How are you doing? Getting anywhere with your case?" He said.

"Well, yes and no, to be honest" he replied. He wasn't sure how much to reveal to this man as he was pretty sure he was the source of the original leak to the press when the first two bodies were found. If it wasn't him directly, then he must have discussed their first conversation with someone else in the pub who took it on themselves to speak to the newspaper.

He couldn't really blame any of them. It was human nature to seek sensationalism and any whiff of a good story, most people couldn't help themselves despite having promised 'I won't tell a soul'. He, Chamberlain should have known better than to confide in him in the first place. In his defence, it had seemed like an open and shut case to begin with.

"Between you and me" he said, and the barman tapped his nose, knowingly, "I think someone has got it in for me personally" there, he had said it. "I shouldn't really be telling you this" he added.

"Oh you can count on me Inspector" replied Jones. "You wouldn't believe the things I get told in here in confidence. There are so many secrets up here" he said tapping his head, "that I have forgotten who told me most of them" he guffawed.

*Yes, I bet* thought Chamberlain, sarcastically.

"Can I ask you a bit more about this lone fella who you told one of my guys about?" Asked the policeman.

"Not sure I can tell you any more really. As I said before, he kept himself to himself. I did try to engage in conversation on one occasion but he didn't seem keen to talk to me" came the reply.

"Didn't you speak to him at all?" asked Chamberlain, a little exasperated.

"Well, beyond asking him what he wanted to drink and taking payment from him, not really. I did ask him where he was from and what he did. All I got was 'from here about's' and "got a relative who owns a farm near here that I help out with' and that was that" recalled Jones.

Chamberlain's ears pricked up. Farm. Relative. Near here. It might be nothing. He might have made it up. But....

He thanked the barman and rushed out, reaching in his pocket for his phone. He got through to his sergeant.

"Tom, pick me up from the high street will you. We need to go looking for a farmer" he shouted at the phone.

Ten minutes later his sergeant pulled up next to him. He jumped in the front passenger seat.

"What's this all about, Sir?" asked Harris.

"What's the name of the farmer that owns the fields and woods around the crime scenes? And where is the farm itself?" Chamberlain blurted out.

"Err, Corrigan....Peter Corrigan" said Harris. "Not sure of the address off the top of my head but it will be in my note book".

Chamberlain looked at him for a few seconds, then when Harris didn't continue, he raised his eyebrows and tilted his head as if to say *And?*

"Left jacket pocket" said Harris eventually.

Chamberlain awkwardly reached into his

sergeants pocket looking for the notebook.

"I have sown a seed. I told the barman that I thought this was all personal to me. I am expecting him to spread this around and hopefully it will get to the newspaper. I know DCI Flemming would not sanction a press release with such details but I want our killer to know that we know what he is about." Chamberlain explained as he retrieved the notebook and started looking through it.

"Ah, got it. Engleston Farm, Old Birmingham Road. Step on it, blue lights Tom" he instructed. "I'll call for back up and an armed response team" he was getting excited. Was this it? Was this the break they needed?

He realised he hadn't really explained to Harris what all the fuss was about so he relayed his conversation with the barman and explained his theory as to who and where the killer might be.

"Have you got that still from the CCTV on your phone, Tom" asked Chamberlain.

"Yup" Harris replied.

They sped through the streets of Warwick, narrowly missing a few wing mirrors but not any pedestrians. Tom was a superb driver and despite not liking being a passenger, Chamberlain was happy to be driven by him.

"Back up can be on the road in 5 minutes so

shouldn't be far behind us" Chamberlain informed his Sergeant, who simply nodded. He was concentrating on the road and any potential obstacles and hazards.

Soon they out of the town itself and heading up the Birmingham Road. The address of the farm was a little farther up than the lay-by opposite the footpath that led to the murder scenes.

"I don't want to spook him so slow it down and lights off when we get near" Chamberlain instructed, as they sped past the lay-by and then the farm track which was the alternative access round the back of the woods. The address they had been given was another half a mile beyond.

Harris slowed the vehicle as they approached the farm, light and sirens off. The farm entrance was quite wide, for tractors presumably but the track was quite rough so it was just as well they had slowed down. After about 150 yards they came to the farmhouse with a large area in front with various agricultural vehicles parked up randomly.

The yard was concreted but was covered in mud, some dry and some wet. Chamberlain could imagine what the wet consisted of. It was a dairy farm after all, at least partially. They came to a stop and carefully got out of the car as a man approached from the direction of some outbuildings to one side of the main farmhouse. Chamberlain recognised the man he had seen and spoken to in the field.

"Your the copper that was asking about my

cows down near the woods where I found those bodies, aren't you? said Peter Corrigan.

"Yes, DI Chamberlain, sir" said Chamberlain. The farmer was not the person in the CCTV. This was disappointing. "Can I ask you if you know or have seen this person in, or around, the area?"

The farmer looked quizzical. "Is this some kind of joke?" He started "That's my young cousin Neil".

His cousin. Helps him out from time to time. Knows the area.

"Is your cousin here at the moment, Mr Corrigan?" asked Chamberlain.

"No, god, I 'aven't seen him for over a year now" replied Corrigan. "Said 'e had some things to sort out and wouldn't be around to help out for a while".

Just then, back up arrived in the form of two marked police cars, a plain black van and an Interceptor vehicle loaded with armed police.

"Bloody 'ell" exclaimed Corrigan. "What's this all about? What's my cousin done? Is he ok?" questioned the farmer.

"Tom, can you?" Indicated Chamberlain. Harris nodded and walked over to the lead vehicle.

"Ok guys, stand down for now" he instructed.

"We need to find your cousin as a matter of

urgency" said Chamberlain to the farmer. "We believe he is responsible for at least 4 deaths".

"Bollocks" said Corrigan. "He can be a bit odd but he ain't no looney killer".

Chamberlain was intrigued that he had used the same phrase as the Professor to describe who they now thought was a serial killing psychopath. It was understandable that a member of the public should use the vernacular but a learned Professor?

Despite what the farmer had told them, they searched the farmhouse and surrounding outbuildings to make sure. In an abandoned farm building, they found a locked room where their killer had been planning his exploits. Pictures of Chamberlain, newspaper cuttings, pictures of Mrs Frobisher and, disturbingly, pictures of Judith Flemming. There was also a camp bed that had clearly been used recently. This all confirmed that Neil Corrigan was the man they were looking for.

It also proved that despite what Peter Corrigan had said, his cousin, Neil, had been around the farm recently, albeit possibly without his knowledge if he was telling the truth. Chamberlain instructed that everything be left as it was. They would leave a team on stake out just in case he came back again. Maybe they would be able to apprehend him and stop the killings. It was a long shot as they had made a bit of a brouhaha when they arrived at the farm so Neil Corrigan would have noticed if he was anywhere in the area. Still, belt and braces.

# CHAPTER 43

Neil Corrigan had been witness to the scene at the farm. He was watching from the woods, waiting for darkness so that he could return to his hidden HQ.

"Well done Inspector, you are well and truly on the trail now" he whispered to himself.

He retreated further into the woods and waited for the police to leave the farm. No doubt they would be watching it so he would have to abandon the shed and go back to his flat. No matter. Things were drawing to a conclusion now anyway.

He should get on with it as soon as possible really. Maybe Chamberlain wasn't as stupid as he had first thought and might spoil the whole plan, like he did that first time. His blood began to boil at the thought of it.

*Not this time, copper* he thought to himself. He would execute the finale and then slip away, like he always did, undetected.

He liked the wood at night, the sounds of nighttime hunters, the rustle of fleeing prey. The natural world was full of the same process all over, so why not for humans? Why not him?

He sat for a while with his back against a tree for support, waiting for darkness. The ground was slightly damp but he didn't notice. His mind was fixed on getting the next few hours correct.

He knew these woods well, the whole area in fact. He had spent much of his latter childhood here, roaming the fields and woodland. This was why he knew The Path so well, and the area with the mounds. It had been an obvious choice for him to bury his earlier victims and now for the scene of Mrs Frobisher's demise.

He knew his oaf of a cousin was also familiar with the area and also roamed about in the course of managing the farm. He would soon discover and report the bodies, both of the poachers and the housekeeper. If they found the other bodies as a result, so be it. He would be moving on after all this so it mattered little to him.

He drifted into a kind of semi-sleep. In his fantasy, he was stalking and killing, stalking and killing, each one more delicious than the last. The faces of his fantasy victims mixed in with the ones of his real victims. A swirl of power and control. Nobody could stop him.

He woke with a start. Some noise had disturbed him. He looked around in the half light, it was still dimpsy. He couldn't identify the noise but he reckoned he should get going. He would have to drive out the long way round so as to avoid any traps the cops may have left. An inconvenience but not the end of the world. An extra 30 minutes or so driving.

After waiting to see if he heard the noise again he decided there was no danger. It was probably a woodland creature starting out on a nights hunting, or one returning to their burrow before they became a victim themselves.

He rose and headed off into the increasing darkness of the wood, in the opposite direction to the farm and the activity there. After about 20 minutes he reached the spot where he had parked his van. The vehicle had been very useful over the last few months, transporting various things. Bodies, in fact.

It would now be put to use to transport a live one. Well, live initially anyway.

# CHAPTER 44

Chamberlain met Judith Webster at the restaurant at 7.30 sharp. They were both on time. Judith had chosen the venue this time and it was quite a large busy eatery on the outskirts of Warwick. He was a little dubious but she assured him the steaks were fantastic.

Once seated at their table, it actually felt quite intimate, despite the size of the place. They ordered a fairly decent bottle of red, and steaks each, both medium rare. Judith sat back and looked straight at Ralph Chamberlain.

"So, where are we going with this?" she asked bluntly.

"Well, I don't know how much Rebecca has told you about the current situation with the case but we have another body. We are pretty confident we have a serial killer, and we think we know who it is." He replied in a very serious tone.

She laughed. Not what he was expecting. "I meant you and me you foolish boy" it was slightly mocking of his naivety.

"Ah, right" he was non-plussed. He wasn't used to this sort of upfront honesty.

She leant over and put her hand on his. It felt good. "I like you Ralph Chamberlain, a lot. I need to know whether you feel the same or whether I am about to, or already have, made an utter twat of myself" she said in a conciliatory manner.

"You're not…you haven't" he said simply. She smiled. The wine arrived, which broke the slightly awkward atmosphere.

"Look, I'm not asking you to marry me tomorrow, neither am I about to jump you after this short a time" she said. "I just want to know if we are at the start of something. Neither of us are kids so we don't have to dance around for weeks trying to establish if the other likes us….do we?"

"No, no I guess not. I suppose I am just a little out of practice and not used to such up front honesty" he explained. *If only I was confident, witty, charming, handsome, rich, attractive, clever…….*

"Does it put you off?" she asked.

"No…it's refreshing actually, once I get over the shock" he said with a slight grin.

While they were verbally sparring, someone was watching from a distance. He was frowning. They were getting on really well. He should be

SIMON FORD

pleased at that because what he was planning would be even sweeter the more they liked each other. But something else was gnawing at his emotions. Was he jealous?

He had followed her from her flat and had decided that he could get away with taking a table in the restaurant, seeing as it was quite a large establishment. He had also taken subtle steps to disguise himself due to his picture being in the papers.

He would sit and wait and if the opportunity arose he would spring into action.

Chamberlain and the journalist were getting on better and better. He was telling her about his recent trip to Barcelona, the architecture and the much better weather.

"I think my next holiday will be somewhere in Eastern Europe" he said. "Budapest, maybe".

"Sounds exotic" she replied. "I haven't been many places to be honest. I did go to New York once with the girls. Very messy and I couldn't tell you anything about the architecture....I don't even remember much about the weather".

They continued the easy flowing chit chat and time slipped by. They had eaten well and drunk moderately. Coffee was being served, with a nice looking mint perched on the saucers.

"Will you excuse me, I need a pee" said Judith. Gone were the days when a lady would refer to it as powdering her nose, apparently.

"Of course" Chamberlain replied.

She got up and headed to the other side of the restaurant and the sign for the toilets. Someone else got up and headed in the same direction. Nothing suspicious in a busy restaurant. Chamberlain certainly didn't notice.

There was a fire exit at the end of the corridor where the toilets were situated. It led out to a quiet street behind the restaurant where a car had been parked, ready for use.

When Judith came out of the ladies, she saw a man by the door who seemed to be having some kind of feinting fit. She went towards him to offer assistance.

"Are you ok there?" She said, helpfully. The man didn't respond so she went right up to him. He glanced up the corridor and saw there was no one there. Like a flash he reared up and put something over her nose and mouth. She felt light headed and then...nothing.

He quietly pushed open the fire escape door and man-handled her outside and over to his car, popped the boot open and folded her inside, then shut the boot. Job done. He drove away, slowly, so as not to draw attention.

How delicious, to have stolen her away from right under his nose, just like the extraction of his housekeeper.

Back at his table, Chamberlain was thinking

she was taking a long time….and her coffee would be getting cold.

"Excuse me, waiter" hailed Chamberlain.

"Yes Sir?" He replied.

"Could you check the ladies for me? My friend went nearly 15 minutes ago and I am a little worried about her" he said.

The waiter went off in the direction of the toilets, returning very quickly.

"There is no one in the ladies toilets at the moment sir" said the waiter.

"What? That can't be right. Are you sure? Said Chamberlain.

"Absolutely sure sir" said the waiter.

Had she had enough and walked out on him? He'd thought they were getting on pretty well. Then he noticed her bag was still slung over the back of her chair. He went icy cold. Surely not.

# CHAPTER 45

DI Chamberlain had searched the whole restaurant and the vicinity outside. There was no sign of Judith Webster. He had rung DCI Flemming first and then his sergeant. The restaurant was now full of police, some in uniform, some CID.

"I think he might have taken her" he'd said to his boss when she arrived.

"We'll find her" she said, rather unconvincingly.

He was shaking and sitting in a chair. He had let his guard down. He had failed her. She was now, possibly, in danger of losing her life to this psychopath who was clearly targeting people close to him. He suddenly thought that he must have been watching them in the restaurant, even been a customer himself.

"Harris, ask the waiting staff if there was a lone male at any of the tables tonight will you? I think he must have been here all along." He said.

Harris went off to question the staff who were hanging around the reception desk. The restaurant had been cleared, much to the annoyance of the clientele. *Tough shit* he'd thought.

Harris returned about five minutes later.

"There was a single occupancy table for two on the other side of the restaurant and the customer disappeared leaving an unfinished meal...." He paused, but clearly had more to say.

"What?" Barked Chamberlain.

"When he booked in, he used the name Ronald Denton." He said.

"Fuck!" exclaimed Chamberlain. "That's him, Neil Corrigan, the bastard has got Judith and it's my fault."

Suddenly Chamberlain's text received noise rang out. He grabbed the phone from his pocket and stared at the notification in disbelief.

"It's from Judith!" He said. But when he read the message it was clear that it was not from Judith Webster. It read...

*Well this is fun eh Inspector? I have your friend, safe and sound, for now. I know you can trace this, and I hope you will. To save your friend you must come to me, on your own. And no cheating, as that would upset me. You don't want to upset me.*

The almost conversational tone made it all the more chilling.

"Tom, get the phone traced, now" ordered Chamberlain.

"You are not going after this lunatic on your own, Ralph" said Flemming.

"I have to. I can't risk Judith's safety" replied Chamberlain. The shaking had stopped and he had a steely look in his eyes that worried his boss somewhat.

DS Harris came off the phone call he was making to tech services.

"They tried the trace immediately but the phone is off with battery removed" he told the group.

"The bastard is buying time. He won't let the trace happen until he is ready. He has control." said Chamberlain.

DCI Flemming got on her phone and Chamberlain could hear her ordering road blocks on all the roads out of Warwick. If he hadn't already, he would find it nearly impossible to get out of town. Hopefully that would narrow the search area. If he had slipped through….

"Right, there is no more we can do here. Back to the station so we can gather the team and make a plan of action" said DCI Flemming.

They all agreed and headed off to their various transport. Chamberlain's mind was racing around, panicking if he was honest. Where can he have taken her? He prayed that Corrigan wouldn't kill her straight away so that they would have a chance to find them. He couldn't bear it if she came to any harm.

Arriving back at the police station, they all convened in the incident room. The station was quiet as all the day time staff had gone home for the night.

"Jesus...where do we start? I can't think straight" said Chamberlain, to no one in particular.

"We keep trying to ping the phone so that we know immediately it is turned on" said Harris, taking the initiative and recognising that his boss was in a state.

"Yes, good, Tom. See that tech get on to us as soon as they have it" replied Chamberlain.

"This maniac has obviously been watching you closely Ralph. And people they consider to be close to you" said DCI Flemming. "Any further thoughts on why they are targeting you?"

"No, not really. Nothing a rational human being would consider worthy of all this. But I guess we are not dealing with a rational person. Do you think your friend Professor Phillips would be up for another chat? I know it's late but we need everything we can get" Chamberlain enquired of his boss.

"I'll ring him now" said Flemming and disappeared off towards her office.

"He risked a lot to grab Miss Webster from right under your nose, Sir" said Harris. "It's as if he couldn't wait and needed to move things along."

"I think this is his finale" said Chamberlain. "He wants me, and he wants to play this out at a place and time of his choosing".

"Do you think he will go back to the path in the woods?" Piped up DC Norrish.

"Good thinking, Norrish. Get uniform and armed response over there to check. Also get them to check the farmhouse and shed. Speak to Peter Corrigan again and tell him what has happened. He may know something that might help us" instructed Chamberlain. His mind was coming back into focus. Move logically, check everything.

DCI Flemming came back into the room.

"Richard was out for a meal in a restaurant not far from here so he is going to come in and speak to us. He insisted" she said.

"That's very kind of him considering the time" said Chamberlain. It was nearly midnight now.

While they waited for the arrival of the Professor and for the uniformed officers to report back on the path and the farm, DC Dixon made them all hot drinks. Not the best quality but sufficient under the circumstances.

Chamberlain was pacing in his office with the door shut and the window open. He was puffing away at his pipe. DCI Flemming decided not to remind him of the no smoking policy inside the station. She knew he needed his pipe right now.

Twenty minutes later, the cll came back from the uniformed officers tasked with checking the Farm and the path. There was nothing there. Peter Corrigan was in disbelief still about his cousin but did tell them that he was a cousin by adoption not by blood.

Maybe that explained why there was no apparent family history that would have made Neil Corrigan into what he was now. Peter had told them that both his and Neil's families had been secure, loving and non-violent. Not what you expect for a psychopathic serial killer. His birth name was Neil Parker. Chamberlain asked DC Dixon to look into the family records and see what the true history was.

Professor Phillips arrived. He was dressed in a very well cut suit and was wearing a rather flamboyant tie.

"I gather your worst fears have been realised Inspector" he said to Chamberlain.

"Yes, very much so. Did Rebecca tell you exactly what has happened?" queried Chamberlain.

"Yes, she did. I am so sorry. Anything I can do or say to help, please ask away." Offered Phillips.

"I need to find this maniac before he hurts anyone else, in particular, Judith. We are waiting for him to turn on her phone so that we can track it. This appears to be what he wants us to do, but in his own time. He has demanded that I go to him, alone" said Chamberlain.

"He is revelling in the control he has over the situation and over you. I suspect he won't hurt her in the meantime. She is the bait. Sorry to be blunt but he will feel no empathy towards her. It's you he is after. Without knowing why it is difficult to know how to play this. It's all about him, a true narcissist. He may not even have an exit plan. All for glory, that sort of thing." The professor paused and appeared to be thinking.

After a moment of two he continued. "It's possible he wants to go out with a bang, figuratively speaking, hopefully. He may chose somewhere spectacular for the finale of his game".

The room went quiet. Chamberlain took all this in and tried to think of places that would fit with that. *The Castle.*

He kept that thought to himself. He knew his boss would never leet him go into this situation on his own without back up. He didn't want to risk anything happening to Judith. He had to go alone.

"So if he hates me so much, why hasn't he just come after me. Why these other deaths?" He asked the Professor.

"He enjoys killing. Plain and simple. The

reasons people kill are many and varied. Why did kill JFK, if indeed he did. Why did Mark David Chapman kill Lennon, how could a mother kill her own children. See killers want control, some attention, some revenge….and some want all of these things."explained the Professor. "By killing someone in your patch, he gets your attention. Then killing someone close to you he demonstrates his control. Then finally, he gets his revenge by killing you. He wants you to come to him, hence Judith as the bait, as a final piece of control".

"You were right when we first met, Professor. A looney killer" said Chamberlain.

"And any revenge motive may be entirely disproportionate. More than likely is, as I can't imagine you have killed anyone Inspector." Added the Professor.

"Not yet" said Chamberlain, darkly.

If he had noticed, the Professor chose to ignore this last comment.

"People either blame themselves when things go wrong, or they blame any and everyone else. A psychopath would fall into the latter category. Which are you Inspector?" Asked Phillips.

"I would say I am a mixture of both. I will admit if I have made a mistake but will also lay blame at others feet where it is justified" replied Chamberlain.

"Then you are very normal" said Phillips with a smile.

Chamberlain had another thought. "And why risk taking her in such a public place? He could have waited until she was in her own home, like Mrs Frobisher".

"Taking her from the restaurant, right under your nose, would have given him immense satisfaction. It was worth the risk in his eyes" said Phillips.

Chamberlain excused himself, claiming he needed the gents. He went straight past the toilets and headed out to the carpark where he had left his Cavalier. He drove off into the night, heading towards the first of his ideas…Warwick Racecourse.

He didn't really know what he would do if he did find Neil Corrigan. He was no action man hero. He just couldn't sit and wait for Corrigan to call the shots. He was good at talking, that was his only real weapon. Not necessarily effective against an unpredictable psychopathic killer. He hoped it would buy him enough time before his colleagues came in mob handed and people….Judith…got hurt. He knew they would have discovered he was missing and be out searching. They would find him very soon.

For some reason he didn't give any thought to his own safcty. It wasn't important. As long as he saved Judith. He couldn't deny that she had got beneath his skin. Would he act differently if it wasn't her in danger? He didn't know the answer to that one.

As he drove away from the police station he was desperately trying to think of places that Corrigan may have taken Judith. Somewhere important, the Professor had said, either to him or to Corrigan. He saw a signpost for the Racecourse and in the absence of any other immediate ideas he headed in that direction.

It didn't mean anything to himself but he suddenly thought about the Cheltenham Racecourse theft so it was possible this racecourse was important to his enemy, or racecourses in general.

He drove along Hampton Street but as he approached the main entrance gates they were firmly shut. He could see no activity or lights anywhere. There wasn't any obvious access point.

As he drove on he noticed a second entrance to the Racecourse Caravan and Motorhome park. He turned into the entrance and slowed his car right down.

Looking around the ghostly park, it was clear there was no one about. There wasn't any racing at the moment so the accommodation caravans would be empty. This was no good. He turned the car and headed back out to the main road.

*Where the fuck else would this lunatic go?* He thought to himself. He must find Judith. He knew from dealing with relatives of missing persons that the feeling they will be found safe never goes away. Hope against hope....whatever the hell that meant....hoping that something would happen even though it seemed impossible he guessed. His mind was wandering and thinking idiotic thoughts. Concentrate.

If the road blocks had done their job, Corrigan must be somewhere within the town. It wasn't a large town so his options would be limited. He thought about the layout of Warwick with the River Avon flowing through it. *The River!* What else was on the river? *The Castle*

He realised he was not that far from Warwick Castle which lay in extensive grounds on the other side of the Stratford Road, which turned into West St and then the High Street. He put his foot down and raced across the town. It should only take a couple of minutes.

Where in the Castle though? It was a huge old building, part of which had recently suffered a fire, the Mill Wheelhouse, and was undergoing repair work. There was also the famous Dungeon, a very popular tourist attraction. Too obvious? Maybe.

He drove at speed up the High St and turned right into Castle St and then left on Castle Lane. His mind was racing. He didn't really notice what he was driving past. It wasn't safe but he didn't have time to worry about that at the moment. He had to find Judith. He had to save Judith. He sounded like a Knight in shining armour. He didn't feel like one, for sure. Part of him wished he was armed.

He didn't really like the idea of all policemen carrying firearms like in a lot of other Countries, probably most other Countries if he thought about it.

But right now he could do with the feeling it might give him to have a weapon in his hand. He was trained on small firearms for emergency situations. This was one of those but he hadn't had tie to go through all the rigmarole of drawing a weapon from the armoury. He would have had to clear it with his DCI for a start.

If he survived the night, she was going to kill him for sneaking off on his own, without back up. He would feel the same if one of his team did the same but he felt he had no choice. They were no idle threats from Neil Corrigan. He would do what he had said he would do if Chamberlain didn't come alone. It was his only chance to resolve the situation and save Judith. This is what he had told himself at any rate.

What he was going to do exactly he didn't know. It would depend on the scenario he found when he got there. It wouldn't be swinging in through the window on a convenient rope or crashing through a wall in his car to save the day. He told himself to stop fantasising and concentrate of driving, fast, and finding this sick murderer.

He drew near to the main Castle entrance. All was dark. During the renovations everything was shut down. There were a couple of vans in the car park, builders vehicles he assumed. Or maybe one belonged to Corrigan?

He parked his car and sat there for a while, just watching and listening. All was quiet. He got out of his car and walked as quietly as he could towards the vans. The first one's engine was cold. The second one, however, was still warm so must have been driven recently. Not conclusive but he was now fairly sure he was in the right place.

It was still some distance to the Castle itself. He jogged as quietly as he could up the access road until he reached the imposing Castle walls.

There wasn't a lot of light but it also was not completely dark. Shadows taunted him at the far reaches of his vision. He told himself to get it together. As he drew close to the main entrance of the Castle he wondered how he was going to gain entrance. Surely it would be all locked up?

He tried the huge oak double doors and discovered he was correct. They didn't budge. *Shit!* He told himself not to panic, there were bound to be other entrances to such a rambling fortress. He decided to move methodically around the walls of the castle… maybe a side door or a window would allow him access, even if he had to force entry.

Rebuilt in stone in the 12th century on the site of the original castle built by William the Conqueror, Warwick Castle is one of the most visited tourist attractions in England. It is huge, and in remarkable condition. Access would be difficult. It was a castle after all.

It had been many years since Chamberlain had visited but when he was young, he loved to come to the Castle and its' grounds. He had become obsessed with the building. Always asking how they had managed to build such a formidable structure in a time when they had no cranes or other plant machinery. It might have sown the seeds of his love of architecture.

Ok, so the Castle was important to him but how the hell would Corrigan know that? He had a sudden chill rush through his body. In pride of place above the mantlepiece in his lounge was a painting of Warwick Castle, in all its' magnificence. Neil Corrigan must have been inside his house.

The chill turned quickly to his blood boiling as he became furious at the thought of the intrusion. This must be the place. *He is in here somewhere!*

*Think* he scolded himself. Where would the weak points be in order to gain access. There must be a Security System in place, CCTV at least and maybe mobile security guards. So far, there had been no sign of such a presence, which was ominous. He thought about his visits all those years ago. The Cafe might provide an easy break in point. He looked at his watch in the semi-light. They would have noticed his absence by now so would soon be out looking for him.

He walked round to the cafe and tried the door. He felt a heavy blow to the back of his neck....then everything went black as he crumpled to the floor.

# CHAPTER 46

Back at the station the team were busy looking at maps, re-visiting statements and generally desperately trying to work out where the killer would have taken his victim. DCI Flemming came back into the incident room.

"Has anyone seen DI Chamberlain recently? I need to have a chat with him" she announced.

Everyone looked up and around the room. He was nowhere to be seen, not even in his corner office.

"He might be outside with his pipe" suggested DS Harris.

"Go and check will you please" said Flemming. She had a worried look on her face.

"M'am" Harris disappeared out of the door and headed to the outside of the building. His gut told him he wouldn't find his boss out there. His gut was right. He rang Chamberlains mobile number. It went to voicemail. *Bugger*.

Harris ran back into the building and up to the incident room, worried about how he was going to tell the DCI what she probably had already guessed judging by the look on her face.

"No sign I'm afraid, M'am" reported Harris.

"Stupid bugger has gone off on his own hasn't he?" she exclaimed. There was silence in the room. "Well? Hasn't he?" shouted the DCI.

"Looks like it, yes M'am" said Harris.

"Bloody idiot" she said. "When I catch up with him…" she didn't finish the sentence. "Can we track his phone, Harris?"

"Yes, M'am, if he has it with him and hasn't taken the battery out, or turned the GPS off" said Harris.

"Get it done, now" ordered the DCI. "Would he even know how to do that?" She added. She knew Chamberlain wasn't the most tech savvy of the team so hopefully he would have it with him and it would be on, and charged up enough to be able to trace.

"Who knows with him, M'am" said Harris. He knew his boss could surprise everyone, even himself, when it came to these things. It depended on whether he wanted to be found. He set about getting the tech people to try the trace.

"I'll request back up from the police helicopter" said Flemming.

She went to her office to make the call. She

came back a few minutes later.

"They have approved the request but it is currently involved in a car chase the other side of Birmingham. Once they have finished there, they will have to refuel so they couldn't give an accurate timescale. We will just have to hope it is soon. They could be invaluable in finding Chamberlain and Judith" she said, sounding frustrated.

In the meantime, Harris tried to think where his boss might have gone. He must have an inkling as to where the killer would be holding Miss Webster. *Think Harris* he told himself. He couldn't just sit at his desk and hoe the phone trace would come up trumps. It might be too late by then. He made a decision. He would probably get into deep shit over it but this was his boss and to a degree, he felt, his friend.

He got up and subtly moved across the room and out of the door. Everyones attention appeared to be taken up elsewhere so no one noticed him leave. He reached the car park and a thought occurred to him. He sent a short text to DC Norrish.

*Car park NOW. Don't tell anyone.*

He really shouldn't do this alone and Norrish would be a great wing man. He just hoped he could get out of the station unseen. A few minutes later, Norrish found him skulking by his car.

"What's going on?" said Norrish.

"Sshh! I am going after Chamberlain and I need

you for back up. It's against orders so if you don't want to come, that's fine. I have to do this anyway." said Harris.

"I'm in" said Norrish, without hesitation. "Where do you think they are?"

"I don't know but I can't just sit there waiting. He had a couple of hours head start on us but I doubt it will be far away. This Corrigan thinks he is in control so may take unnecessary risks. Let's just get out there and start looking"

They both got in the car and Harris drove out of the station car park, wondering what the hell he was doing, and where the hell they were going. He turned right, for the sake of going somewhere. This took them along Northgate and into Priory Road. A quick drive around Priory Park wouldn't do any harm. A large expanse of mostly woods with the Priory in the middle. It was opened in 1953 as an urban park offering an interpretive nature trail, specimen trees & wildlife.

"Keep a sharp look out for the Boss's car" ordered Harris. "And anything suspicious" he added.

"What do you mean by suspicious?" queried Norrish.

"I don't know!" shouted Harris. "Use your nouse!"

They drove around the park but the journey

was fruitless. No sign of their boss's car...no sign of anything. Harris decided to try the Racecourse. It wasn't far but involved going back to Northgate and then up the A425 and turning left at the big roundabout and down Theatre Street. There was little or no traffic at that time of night so their progress was quick.

Harris put his foot down. He didn't want to put the blues and twos on as he didn't want to warn Corrigan. He turned right into Linen Street and sped towards the Eastern side of the racecourse. He drove around the perimeter, heading South towards the Hampton Road Car Park. He couldn't think of where else to go.

They were, once again, disappointed on their arrival. Time was slipping away and they were wasting it.

"Shit" exclaimed Harris, slamming his hand on the steering wheel. "Now would be a good time for any bright ideas, Norrish".

"Are we sure he would have stayed in Warwick Sarge?" Asked Norrish.

"No. But where the fuck else do we look. If not in town then there are thousands of places he could have taken the woman" . Harris slumped his head down on the steering wheel.

"THE CASTLE" he exclaimed suddenly. "Why didn't you think of that before Norrish?" Accused Harris, knowing full well it was himself who should have thought of it and it was unfair to accuse his junior of a lack of foresight.

There was a faint hint of dawn in the East now. Morning was approaching and it had been 3 hours since they had noticed their boss was missing. Harris had a churning in his stomach. A feeling of foreboding that he couldn't shift.

He sped out of the car park and straight across the A4189 and into Goldsmith Avenue. Traffic was starting to get heavier and the town was waking up with the associated noises filling the air. His route led him across to the Stratford Road where he turned left, accelerating up towards Warwick Castle.

There were many places within the Castle grounds that could be where the action was playing out, let alone the huge Castle itself. It could take hours to search the whole area. Harris would have to take a gamble. He probably only had one shot at this.

He screamed into the car park and immediately saw Chamberlain's vehicle, parked near a couple of vans. Ok, so this was where they needed to be. Time to call in the cavalry. As he got out of the car he shouted to Norrish to call it in and get back up, ASAP.

He went over to his boss's car and felt the bonnet. Cold. He must have been there for some time. God knew what had been happening in that time. He hoped he wasn't too late.

"I'm going in" he said to DC Norrish who had just come off the radio. "You wait here and guide the troops in".

"But Sarge…" protested Norrish but his sergeant was already on his way to the main Castle entrance and ignored him.

Like Chamberlain, he found the main doors well and truly shut. Unlike Chamberlain, he found the first accessible window, smashed it and made his entrance to the building. They could take the repair cost out of his wages. It was dark inside but he had his maglite torch and switched it on. It was eery being in the old castle when no one else was around. Although there was a faint hint of dawn outside, it was still pretty dark inside the Castle.

The place was cold and smelled of 'old', mixed with a hint of modern polish. He tried to remember the layout of the Castle from the times he had been on guided tours of the place. It was a huge building and would take ages to search the whole thing on his own.

He remembered there was a dungeon that was very popular with visiting tourists. A macabre interest but then that was what people were like. Torture, murder, war….all things that fascinated people for some reason. The reality of all those things was actually horrible and people might realise that if they came face to face with the real thing.

Harris made his way forward. He found a stand full of leaflets and cast his torch beam over them. *Yes, a map of the Castle.* He grabbed the map and unfolded it, searching for the dungeon. He headed in the direction indicated. Was is too obvious? A cliche? That the final confrontation would be in the dungeon of a medieval castle....just like in the movies?

As he made his way through the castle he checked all the rooms he passed. All dark and empty.

"Norrish, come in" he said quietly into his radio.

"Receiving sarge" came the rather loud reply. He turned the volume down a bit on the receiver.

"I'm going to check the dungeon Norrish. I'll let you know if I find anything".

"Copy that sarge. Back up is on the way, probably 5-6 minutes. Flemming was not happy".

*I bet she wasn't* thought Harris. He continued on. The dye were cast now, too late to withdraw.

He got to The Great Hall with its' impressive displays of armour, the biggest in England outside the Royal Armouries or the Tower Of London. He passed by the mounted Knights bristling with weaponry. Maybe he should grab a sword or a lance? Maybe not, he might set off an alarm or send a fake horse crashing to the ground together with its' mount.

The map showed the dungeon to be down some steps at the other end of a corridor leading off the far end of the Great Hall. He moved forward, listening for any sound as he went. Nothing. *That horse just winked at me....don't be ridiculous Harris!* he admonished himself.

As he went passed the last window in the hall, he glanced out and thought he saw a glimmer of light.

What was over there? He looked at the plan and saw that it would be the Castle Mill. How did he get to that? The map was unclear as to whether they were connected. He moved on, looking for any connecting corridors or doors. He found what he was looking for. A large wooden door which, when he tried it, started to open. There were large bolts and a drop bar that should have been securing it from being opened from the other side. These had been undone. He was in the right place. He pushed the door fully open.

"Norrish, no need to respond but FYI I am heading into the Castle Mill. Follow with back up as soon as you can" he said into his radio, very quietly. There was a double click in response so he knew Norrish had got the message.

Quietly he entered the Mill House. He could hear the faint murmur of voices from somewhere above.

# CHAPTER 47

DC Norrish was waiting nervously by their car, having received and acknowledged his sergeant's last message. He wished back up would hurry up and get there. He felt powerless.

He heard vehicles approaching. They came in silent, i.e. no blues and twos, as requested by Norrish. The first car to pull up to him contained DCI Flemming. She didn't look very happy. She wasn't. Norrish was about to receive the initial blast of her displeasure. She got out of the car.

"Norrish, what the fuck is going on?" although she whispered these words, they were nonetheless terrifying to Norrish.

"DS Harris has gone in, looking for DI Chamberlain, M'am. He told me to wait here for your arrival. I think he has discovered where they are and could do with back up as soon as possible" said the nervous Norrish.

DCI Flemming grunted and turned to the vehicle behind her, out of which were getting the armed response officers, brandishing various

THE WOODLAND PATH MURDERS

weapons and decked out in protective gear. One of them handed her a protective vest. She briefed the senior officer as to the situation and where they needed to get to in the Castle.

In turn the officer briefed his men. They moved towards the Castle entrance. Again, they found the main door well and truly locked up but they quickly found the window through which Harris had gained access. One by one they made their entrance to the building.

"You and I will follow this team at the rear" ordered Flemming to Norrish. "Whatever happens, we do not go in front of them, is that understood?"

"Yes M'am" replied Norrish. He was already wondering what sort of trouble he was going to be in for sneaking off with the Sarge. He had no intention of trying any heroics, that was for sure.

Once inside the Castle, the armed team of armed men moved forward following a series of hand signals from their senior officer. Flemming and Norrish followed quietly behind. Progress was slow as they had to clear every room they passed. They couldn't rely solely on the intel they had, second hand from Norrish.

Flemming knew some of these men and also knew she had to trust to their training and skill to get the job done. Despite that, it was frustratingly slow getting through the Castle towards where she knew that 2 police officers and 1 civilian were in serious danger. It was made worse by the fact that the civilian was a very dear and close friend of hers. She found herself praying, to what or who she wasn't sure. She couldn't say she believed in a God, or was religious in any way to be honest. However, it was worth a try, wasn't it?

"Why aren't there any security guards on duty here?" She asked, herself more than anyone really. "And where is that bloody helicopter?"

# CHAPTER 48

Chamberlain had been struggling against the cable ties that restrained him. They were a thick version, and not the releasable kind, so he realised he was unlikely to be able to free himself from them, not even stretch them enough to slip his hand through. They were looped through some kind of ring embedded in the old castle wall, next to a solid looking door that obviously led into the castle. It might be possible to loosen the ring enough to pull it out.

When he had come to, he had found himself on some kind of balcony or battlement of the old castle. It overlooked the river, about 40 feet below. He could hear the water rushing over the weir. There was an overturned wheelbarrow lying close to him, presumably how Corrigan had transported him here having knocked him out. He felt cold and there was a smell of damp moss in the air.

Neil Corrigan was standing near to the battlements. He was dressed in black, wearing leather gloves and a black woollen skull cap. He had obviously been waiting in the shadows for Chamberlain before hc knockcd him out.

"So, Detective Inspector. I wanted you to see

what it was that you interrupted all those years ago. I don't like being interrupted." sneered Corrigan.

"What the hell are you talking about?" Chamberlain growled.

"What....not worked it out yet Inspector? You are very slow, you know. Ok, I'll remind you what you did. About 10 years ago we were both just setting out on our separate careers. You as a policeman and me....well, you know what I like to get up to. I had found, followed and trapped what was to be my first. They say you never forget your first, don't they?" He sneered. "I was about to reach the climax of the project when who comes along and puts their size 11s right into it? Yes, you, the young overzealous young copper, out on the beat and keen to make his mark. I had to make my escape PDQ. They made you out to be a hero.....huh, hero indeed. I was not pleased I can tell you, and swore I would get my own back one day" he said. A dark look came over his face. "Everything in my life went to shit after that night. I was thrown out of home, lost my job and ended up living on the streets".

"I think you have the wrong person. I have no idea what you are talking about" said Chamberlain, actually, remembering the scene all too well. He had saved somebodies life that night.

"Don't you dare deny it" snarled Corrigan. He was getting angry now. The whole point was for DI Chamberlain to understand what he had done and suffer the consequences. "You know damn well what you did".

"Nope". He was trying to remember the advice from Professor Phillips about how to communicate with a psychopath. It was all very well in a class room, but face to face was a whole new ball game. *Don't play into the psychopaths game. Steer the conversation back to him.*

"If you've touched her….." The implied threat died on his lips.

"Oh, you mean did I fuck her?" taunted Corrigan. "No, no, fear not, she is not my type. Too skinny, to be honest. I like a bit more to get hold of, if you know what I mean. And anyway, that was not the purpose of taking her".

"I'm not interested in your lascivious sexual habits, you freak" spat Chamberlain.

He looked across the space  at Judith Webster who was not looking in a good state. Corrigan had her suspended by her wrists from a rope that was slung over a high beam that projected out of the castle wall. Her feet only just touched the floor. Her arms and shoulders must have been in agony and she appeared to be drifting in and out of consciousness. Other than that, she looked beautiful. He hadn't touched her. Yet.

"Why her? Why not string me up and kill me if you blame me for everything?" asked Chamberlain.

"All in good time. I wanted to put on a little show for you first." Replied Corrigan. "You know by now that I am responsible for the *Tragic Poacher's Feud* as they described it in the paper, and the demise of your Housekeeper. I have to thank the poacher for introducing me to the snare garrotte. I have made some of my own. These are made from old steel guitar strings. Very easy to turn into a snare. The brass ring at one end is ideal for slipping the wire through. All I really had to do was fix a peg onto the other end". He seemed very proud of his achievement.

Chamberlain could only imagine the horror of what this beast intended to do to the woman, he now realised, he was falling for, big time. Was that even possible in such a short time? He struggled against the metal loop some more and felt a little movement. He tried again. More movement.

"How do you know there aren't teams of police and armed response on their way?" He asked.

"Oh they would have been here by now. You have been unconscious for over an hour and I haven't turned the phone on yet. I didn't need to as somehow you found me, so they can't trace the location. I think you were a sensible boy and came on your own, as directed." said Corrigan.

Unfortunately he was right. Chamberlain had played the lone ranger, something he may now regret. He wasn't entirely sure what he would do if he did

THE WOODLAND PATH MURDERS

get free but he had to try. He looked around the space they were in. It was some kind of battlement with castellations running around the edge. He could hear water flowing beyond them, presumably the river.

"What about the security systems here, how did you get past them?" Keep him talking, thought Chamberlain.

"Ah yes, that was a little tricky. There is now a small group of Security Guards asleep in one of the entrance towers across the courtyard. They will be fine, maybe a little groggy when they wake up. I 'invited' them all, with a little diversion I created, to join me there, and then exposed them to a large amount of chloroform. Works wonders, you know. I couldn't do much about the cameras, but I will be long gone by the time the footage is reviewed. Ironic really. I took the keys from one of the guards and accessed the security room. I watched you arrive and followed your progress so I knew exactly where to ambush you" Corrigan sounded very smug about his successful breach of the Castle's defences.

Chamberlain remembered entering the castle through the main gate, walking across the courtyard towards the cafe and then it all went black. When he came round, he had a very sore head and assumed he had been hit from behind and his hands were restrained behind him and attached to something.

"The show won't take long. I find my projects don't usually last very long once they have the wire tight around their neck." Explained Corrigan, with a certain amount of twisted glee.

So, he planned the same fate for Judith as for his other victims and he expected Chamberlain to watch. He pulled again and the metal hoop appeared to come out of its' seat slightly. He felt a glimmer of hope and tried to think of a plan.

"You know, when I saw you and Miss Webster that first night in the restaurant, I was angry. I had hoped that she was going to give you a hard time but it soon became clear that you were both enjoying yourselves too much. She obviously liked you. So, you see, it is really your fault that she finds herself in her current predicament. She was the bait that I needed to draw you to me" taunted Corrigan.

"You sick bastard" growled Chamberlain.

"Now, now. Language Timothy" said the killer, mimicking the Ronnie Corbett sit com, Sorry. Chamberlain was not going to respond with 'sorry Mother'. His captor was fiddling with a snare, similar to the ones found around the poacher's and Mrs Frobisher's necks. It had a spike on one end, presumably to drive into Judith's neck to secure it, as before. Not that she would be in a position to try to remove it as she was strung up to the beam projecting out of the wall.

"You are sick though, you know that" accused Chamberlain. He was buying time by engaging in this fruitless argument.

"Well, it's subjective really, don't you think?" replied Corrigan, who was still fiddling with the home made snare. "Some, like you, would say I was sick. Others, similar to me, would say I was enlightened and free from societal and cultural boundaries"

"What about moral and legal ones?" countered Chamberlain.

"Both are products of the society and culture that I am free from…..it's pointless, you know"

"What is?" asked Chamberlain. He suddenly realised that Corrigan had already placed a snare loosely around his neck. If he was going to get himself and Judith out of this, he was going to have to summon all his strength, what he had left any way. He still felt a little dizzy from the blow on the head.

"This idiotic attempt to delay me by engaging in some kind of philosophical debate. You know damn well that we will never agree with each other"

*You're damn right on that* thought Chamberlain.

"You have no answer to that by the sounds of it. Oh well, we had better continue" said Corrigan, ominously, and turned his attention back to his preparations.

Chamberlain gave another tug and felt the hoop come free from the wall. He rose from his uncomfortable crouched position and launched himself across the space between him and Corrigan.

"Aaaaaaarrrrrrghhhh" he roared as he closed the distance between them. He barrelled right into Corrigan's stomach, winding him. He continued the charge with as much force as he could. The two men hit the battlements and the force toppled them over the top and they plunged down towards the water below. He could see the surprise in Corrigan's face, which was inches from his. This quickly turned to anger but the momentum of the charge gave Corrigan no opportunity to counter attack or even defend himself.

It wasn't a great plan but it was all he could think of to get Corrigan away from Judith. His hands were still tied behind his back so all he could do was take a deep breath before they hit the water. Corrigan was still winded and was unable to draw breath before going under. Chamberlain fell on top of Corrigan and managed to maintain this position, forcing his foe deeper under water.

Just as they had disappeared over the wall, there was a crash and the door burst open. Harris charged through, saw Judith but no one else. He heard the splash and realised what must have happened. Without breaking a step, he shrugged off his jacket and launched himself over the battlements after his boss.

Harris hit the water not long after the other two but when he surfaced he could see no one else. He dived under the water and tried to search for his boss. He found him lying on top of Corrigan on the gravel bottom of the river. If there had been a struggle, the man underneath was only twitching slightly by the time Harris got to them and grabbed his Boss's jacket and started to haul him to the surface.

When they broke through to the air above, Harris was relieved to hear Chamberlain gasping for air. By now they were nearer to the other bank so he dragged Chamberlain over there and pushed him out of the water.

"Get these bloody cable ties off me Harris" spluttered Chamberlain.

"No worries....and my pleasure by the way" said Harris sarcastically, as he got himself out of the water.

"Yeah, of course, thank you Tom. Impeccable timing. What about Judith?" he queried, sounding very concerned. She had not looked good when he saw her last.

"There was DCI Flemming, DC Norrish and several armed officers behind me Sir, so I'm sure they will have taken care of her. Let's get you freed and we can get over there" DS Harris produced a pocket knife out of his soaking wet trousers and cut the restraints, freeing Chamberlains arms.

"How did you know, Tom?" asked Chamberlain, as he rubbed his wrists and rolled his shoulders to relieve the cramp that had formed.

"Long story but essentially we saw your car in the castle car park and I started a search. I saw a flickering light and was about to enter the Castle Mill when I heard a blood curdling scream....well, a roar really... so I ran up the stairs and charged the door. I must have broken through just as you hit the water because I heard the splash. Two and two, as they say, I just ran after you, and jumped, not much thought about it to be honest." Explained Harris.

"You shouldn't be doing that sort of thing in your condition....well you know what I mean, responsibilities and so on" said Chamberlain. Harris had looked at him quizzically. "Anyway, thank you again. I don't think Corrigan will be surfacing. I am pretty sure I winded him when I charged into him. And then I held him down until he ran out of the little air he had in his lungs....fucking bastard" he almost spat the final words.

They both looked across the water but could see no sign of the man. The police dive team would no doubt have to retrieve him if he didn't float to the surface. Chamberlain was pretty certain he was dead. He had watched the last few bubbles escape from his mouth and the light go from his eyes.

In some ways, death was too good for him. No court appearance, no justice meted out to him, no long prison sentence. However, Chamberlain reckoned the world was a better place without him.

As he stood to make his way to the other side of the river, he realised he had escaped death himself. If it hadn't been for the quick actions of his sergeant, he may well be at the bottom of the river still on top of Neil Corrigan.

Just then, they heard the thwump, thwump, thwump of a helicopter overhead and a great bright light illuminated the scene.

### Epilogue

Judith Webster spent a few days in hospital after her ordeal. She had been weak and dehydrated. Physically she recovered well. The mental scars might take a little longer. She had been given as long as she needed off work. She would certainly have something to write about when she felt strong enough. It would probably be cathartic to write about how she was abducted, used as bait, threatened with garrotting and then rescued by her hero policeman.

Once he had dried out from his dip in the river, and had a few bowls worth of smokes, Chamberlain was right as rain, albeit with a large bruise on the back of his head. He had saved Judith, and Harris had saved him. Initially they couldn't find Corrigan's body and there was a worry that he hadn't perished but had escaped. However, 3 days later his body was found about a mile further downstream, caught on a branch that overhung the water. He was definitely dead.

They found an address on Neil Corrigan's

driving licence in his wallet which was in one of his pockets. On investigation, they discovered that was where he had been living recently. A small flat on the outskirts of Warwick. It was almost bare, very tidy, with very few possessions. They did find a bag with about £1,500 pounds worth of cash in it. They also found a very smart suit, with the receipt in the pocket, traced where it had been bought and filled in some more gaps in the recent life and history of Neil Corrigan. The purchase was recent but they couldn't work out why he had spent so much on the suit. Maybe he had used it as part of a disguise at some point. They would probably never know. He seemed to have been paying cash for everything he bought. He had no credit or debit cards, or even a bank account that they could find.

The bloody clothes he had worn for the poacher's feud murders were found stuffed under a loose floorboard. There was DNA from both victims on the clothing. This was more evidence that tied him to those killings.

———-

DI Chamberlain had gone up to the university to thank Professor Phillips in person. He had vowed to learn more about Criminology and ailments of the mind. The Professor had said he was welcome to sit in on any lectures he fancied. He would.

"I still have some outstanding questions" Chamberlain said to the Professor. He had relayed the whole conversation with Corrigan at the Castle to the Professor.

"I'm not surprised" came the reply.

"For example, why didn't Corrigan bury Mrs Frobisher? Or the poachers?" asked Chamberlain.

"I suspect they were direct messages to you. The other bodies were not part of the bigger project….you!" answered Phillips.

"And his motive seemed to be based on something I wasn't even aware of, so what kind of revenge is that?" came another question from Chamberlain.

"It's not just simple revenge, of which we can all suffer from feelings of, it's obsession and compulsion. He probably felt wronged, in that you had interrupted his 'project' and the thoughts of revenge had grown over the years to the point of obsession" said Phillips. "Nobody said psychopathic serial killers were always rational".

"For someone who seemed to be so proud of his plan, his project, he made some very stupid mistakes. I was weak but I still managed to pull the fixing out of the wall. If I hadn't, I don't know what would have happened. I guess I wouldn't have got wet and Harris would have had to confront Corrigan, one to one." Chamberlain postulated.

"Well, I suspect Corrigan's obsession got the

better of him. He got careless. Lucky for you, unlucky for him" said Phillips.

They swapped personal contact details in case there was anything else Chamberlain wanted to discuss, either about this case or anything in the future.

"Give my love to Rebecca will you" said Phillips. "And keep an eye on her please. I'm a bit worried about her, she looked a bit peaky last time I saw her".

"For sure" agreed Chamberlain. He had had similar thoughts about his boss but had kept them to himself. He hoped she was alright.

———

DS Harris got a commendation for saving Chamberlain's life. He was very proud of this, though said anyone would have done the same. There would be a ceremony in due course, at which some top brass would present him with the award and wax lyrical about bravery, honour and service and such ethereal concepts.

He discussed marriage with Mads and they agreed that maybe they would at some point but there was no hurry. They started the process of arguing about names for their unborn child. Harris was keen on a traditional Warwickshire name, like William for a boy or Elisabeth for a girl but Mads was a little more modern. She liked Brad for a boy or Amelia or Mia for a girl. Although he didn't admit it to her, Tom did think that Brad Harris or Mia Harris had certain rings to them.

———-

When Judith was feeling up to it, Chamberlain asked her out to dinner again. She suggested he come to her place and she would cook. Less likely to get abducted apparently.

They had a very pleasant meal of homemade lasagne and nearly two bottles of Merlot. They talked and talked until late in the evening. She said she didn't blame him for what had happened but he did blame himself. He should have known she was in danger and should have steered clear of her. Corrigan would not then have targeted her and used her as bait.

"You couldn't have known what he would do" she excused him. "Anyway, you're such a good cop you found and rescued me in the nick of time…my hero".

"I don't know about that" he paused for a few moments. "Life was so much simpler when we were young, don't you think?" Judith looked at him with a quizzical expression. "There is a song lyric, Bob Seger I think. 'I wish I didn't know now what I didn't know then'. " He looked at her.

"Who?" she said.

Inwardly he felt it was more luck than judgement but he decided to let her hang on to the hero thing for a bit. It would do him no harm in their blossoming relationship. He hadn't felt like this for so long that he wasn't quite sure what to do next, how to progress things. She took the decision out of his hands.

"So, Inspector, are we going to have sex or what?" said the clearly much better Judith, with a glint in her eye.

Chamberlain didn't go home at all that night.

———-

The Bell & Tankard held a bit of a wake for the two poachers, Ron & Charley. More than just the after work drinkers came along, the nature of funeral gatherings where people come out of the woodwork having 'known the deceased well'. There were some family members as well.

Chamberlain and Harris popped in for one drink to show solidarity with the community. Rob Jones saw them and came over for a quick chat.

"DI Chamberlain, good to see you, though obviously not under the circumstances. I hear you got your man" he said

"Yes, we did. And thank you for your contribution to the investigation" said Chamberlain.

"No problem Inspector" he replied. "Civic duty and all that. And pop in anytime, I'll stand you a pint" Jones nodded at the pair and went off to serve more mourners.

Chamberlain and Harris left them to it. They had also done their civic duty by showing the face of the law.

There was a small, quiet service for Mrs Frobisher at the Warwick Crematorium which was south of Warwick, just off the M40 at Oakley Wood. There would be a memorial plaque for her there, next to her husband's. Chamberlain went on his own. There were very few people there as she had no family. The small group of women, Chamberlain assumed were members of her Bridge Club. They all seemed very shocked and there were tears. Mrs Frobisher had clearly been a popular member of the club.

Chamberlain was both sad and angry at the same time. She had not deserved such a brutal fate. He was glad Neil Corrigan was dead but part of him would have liked to see him go through the justice system, appear in court and be put away for the rest of his life.

There was another funeral later the same week. Neil Corrigan was buried in the Municipal Graveyard in the Pauper's section. Apparently he hadn't wanted to be cremated. Part of his narcissistic nature probably, wanting something physical to be left behind after his death. Warwick Graveyard is, ironically, on the old Birmingham Road a little way out of town before you get to the main A46 Warwick Bypass.

"Do you want to go with me?" Chamberlain asked Judith Webster.

"I'll pass on that, I think" she replied. "Just make sure he is dead and buried for good" she added.

"I know he was an evil bastard but you have to wonder how much he suffered as a child to make him into what he was" offered Chamberlain.

"We have all been battered, not necessarily physically, maybe emotionally, at some point in our lives" she replied. "But it doesn't turn us all into fucking looney killers" she was a little cross at his seeming defence of the man who had nearly killed them both.

*There's that phrase gain, looney killer* Chamberlain mused.

There were two people at the burial, in addition to the officiate. DI Ralph Chamberlain and Peter Corrigan, the deceased's cousin. It was raining, of course.

"Well, Inspector. I'm sorry for the trouble my little cousin caused. Is that young lady ok now?" he asked Chamberlain as they stood by the grave.

"Not your fault Mr. Corrigan. Families, eh?" replied the Inspector, sardonically. "And she is much better, thank you for asking".

Corrigan simply nodded in reply. They stood in silence for a while longer, in the rain.

"Well, that's that then" said Corrigan and

started to walk away.

Chamberlain fell in beside him as they walked through the graveyard toward the exit.

"Did you know about the Iron-age burial mounds in the woods, Mr Corrigan?" asked Chamberlain.

"Oh yeah, 'course. We used to play around them as kids. Didn't really know what they were, mind. We would fantasise that they were sleeping dragons, or buried Kings...that sort of thing. You know what kids are like Inspector." replied Corrigan. "Spooky to think they have been used more recently for nefarious purposes" he added.

Chamberlain did know what they were like, he had been one himself, once. He couldn't quite reconcile the picture of kids in their halcyon days, playing typical kids games over dead bodies, then one of those kids turning out to be a psychopathic serial killer. He'd have to work on that one.

On his way home he thought about Peter Corrigan's use of the word 'nefarious'. It seemed incongruous for a farmer to be using such language. He castigated himself for his stereotyping. He drove home, puffing on his pipe. He thought he would get his "Oom Paul' out later for a nice mellow smoke, listen to Genesis, probably fall asleep in his armchair and more than likely burn another pair of trousers.

———

Warwick Castle appointed a new Security Company to upgrade their systems. They installed new security cameras both within key buildings and across the grounds to protect the attraction from unauthorised access. The project was broken down into two phases.

The first objective was to protect key areas within the 'heart 'of the castle, including The Great Hall, Queen Anne's Bedroom, The Blue Boudoir, The Red Drawing Room and The Cedar Drawing Room, and, of course, the Castle Mill. This part of the solution was accomplished through careful positioning and installation of state of the art Avigilon Megapixel cameras.

The second phase saw the installation of additional Avigilon Megapixel Cameras to monitor the perimeter. This involved video transmission distances of up to 1 kilometre, in effect acting as a digital 'moat 'to protect Warwick Castle's 1100 years of history.

———-

DCI Flemming's biopsy result had been inconclusive for some reason. She had to have further investigations. She had already had various scans and x-rays following the initial breast examination. In her head she knew the answer but there was always hope. Indeed, even if it definitely was breast cancer, modern treatments were much more effective these days and could give a much better prognosis. When she had told her husband, he had broken down in tears and they had an emotional evening talking through the diagnosis. Now, he was being as supportive as he could be. They had decided not to tell their children until they knew more, either way.

She may have more of a future than she first thought. But what about her job? She could probably take early retirement. The stresses of her position wouldn't help her recovery process. Well, she would have to wait until she knew for sure either way.

She had decided not to castigate her team too much. Luckily all had worked out ok. Their behaviour would have to be included in the reports and there would be questions but through a little creative thought, communication problems and timing issues, she managed to avoid any serious repercussions for them. They had been through enough.

Privately, though, one to one she had read the riot act. Mostly to DI Chamberlain as the senior officer. He understood, and she understood why he had acted as he did. Judith was her friend, and now, it would appear, she was more than a friend to Chamberlain.

_____

A few days later back at the station, Chamberlain got a suspicious knowing wink from his boss. He ignored her, thinking better of trying the 'Piss Off' speech again. No doubt Judith had gone into salacious detail about the night they had spent together. He didn't care. It had been great.

He was sitting in his office, wishing he

could get away with lighting his pipe indoors again....thinking how proud of his team he was. He had thought he had noticed something slightly off about his boss, DCI Flemming, but couldn't put a finger on it.

"Sir, a call from Cheltenham nick asking if we have had any luck finding their thief. What shall I tell them?" asked DC Dixon.

Chamberlain simply titled his head to one side and raised his eyebrows.

"On it, Sir" said Dixon, returning to the call.

————-

*He sat propped up against his favourite tree, in his favourite bit of woodland at his favourite time of the day, or rather night. It was gone midnight, the moon was out in full, casting shadows in a silvery light. The owl was calling and the foxes screaming like distressed babies. They were all hunting.*

*The police thought that the killing was over and the murderer was dead. Well, they were right to a degree. His young cousin had gone too far, taken too many risks. He'd got caught, he'd got killed. His vendetta had got the better of him and he had forgotten the importance of his own survival.*

*It had been his own arrogance, and offence at the intrusion, that had made him report his initial discovery of the poacher's bodies. His cousin had overstepped the mark. He was rather annoyed that his childhood playground, with its' mysterious woods and mounds, was now a busy crime scene and archaeological site. They were finding all sorts of evidence of ancient settlement there, let alone his hiding place for his victims.*

*Peter Corrigan was more careful than his cousin had ever been, more experienced. He would have to be more wary now, due to Neil's idiotic campaign against that policeman. He would have to be more ingenious and find another disposal site. The old burial mounds had been ideal camouflage. Not only was the path barely used but there were ancient mounds there already. Perfect.*

*When his cousin had come to him some six months earlier, Peter had decided to put a hold on his own exploits which were rather niche and not time sensitive, other than his own urges. It had been amusing watching things play out. Now, though, he was free to start again....to start hunting again.*

# THE DI CHAMBERLAIN CASES

A series of books about a Warwickshire detective, DI Ralph Chamberlain.

## The Woodland Path Murders

DI Chamberlain and his team work out of Warwick Police Headquarters. A psychopath is on the loose and wants revenge against Chamberlain for something he did as a young policeman.

## The Copse Murders

DI Ralph Chamberlain has another psychopath to deal with. This one is on a vigilante revenge mission aginst organised crime.

# ABOUT THE AUTHOR

## Simon Ford

Born in Surrey in South East England, Simon now lives in Devon. For the last 15 years he ran a Music Festival. Now in his 60s he has turned to writing, firstly about his experience starting and running the festival, and now a series of books about DI Ralph Chamberlain.

Printed in Dunstable, United Kingdom